Quintbridge

Dedicated to my Tayta and all my other loving family and friends.

Thank you for making this possible.

Quintbridge

By Jake Schattin

CHAPTER I

During the nighttime, when the sky was dark and absent of stars by the fault of the cloudy weather, the Shabah family rode by carriage away from their hometown of Fiddlefield. They travelled for many hours, humming tunes that sounded like the howls of the wind, and watching for the possibility of a sunrise. The world seemed to only brighten, though, never casting a beautiful orange or pink in the skies, and, at around noon, Gabriel Shabah took out his diary to scribble some thoughts about his move from Fiddlefield to this new place.

"A godawful neighborhood it seems, absolutely riddled with people drowning in grotesque amounts of money and the superficial. I am not sure how I am supposed to survive a desolation of a town like this one, where everyone is incredibly unlikeable and despicable! Well, I haven't met the townspeople here yet, but soon I will, and afterward, I will make certain to update. Currently, we are still traveling from Fiddlefield to our new home, and it has been a few sleepless hours that I have endured. We should be arriving in a few moments, and I am quite nervous, but also excited—an unexplainable feeling. The twentieth century is upon us, and I feel it might be the best year yet—1900, so many possibilities!"

Gabriel and his family arrived in Quintbridge, a neighborhood that was boldly differentiated by its lavish culture and wealthy population. On appearance, Quintbridge is blotted with trees extending far into the air, absorbing most of the sunlight and casting elephantine shadows across the grounds. The dark green and brown colors mixed within the barks and leaves force the visibility of the neighborhood to be relatively lower than usual, where days are slightly dimmer, and nights are incredibly darker. The roads were constantly repaved, smoothly meandering and winding about as they pleased. In the center of the neighborhood, where the roads and trees encircle, is a dark pond where happy fish the size of a forearm may be found. The pond was always a calm sight, being flat and smooth unlike the rest of the upshooting rocky terrain surrounding the majority of it. The moon caused no waves, and the ripples only slightly grazed against the rocks on the edge of the water. It was a perfectly simple pond for such an overpowering and complicated geography.

Castle-like houses were constructed over consistently measured plots of land, each spanning a few acres out from the road. They all had similar builds—spires, rectangular rooms, patterns of brick, stone, and mahogany, and complex architecture—and were all quite large. Rumors of the women in Quintbridge had circulated around the country, describing them as majestic and regal—the most beautiful women found on the globe. The men had been rumored, too, as ambitious folk when they were young and flourishing into successful employers once they reached the ripe age of twenty-five. All would be rich or famous or powerful, and so it was grand luck that you encounter and befriend any of these men in the future so you could take advantage of their connections. The talking contributed to the neighborhood's renowned fame. The central reason why Ms. Shabah had decided to move here was rooted in these talks. She sold her home in Fiddlefield immediately for the space that had opened up—an old couple had just died, and the local bank left the estate for auction where she bid until she won. She also had decided to move because Gabriel had almost finished with his last year of homeschool and she sought a place to provide him with comfort when he takes a break.

Quintbridge was also the name of the small town that it lies in. The neighborhood seemed consistent with the town's aesthetic, save for the neighborhood's significant dimness. The town holds an expensive farmers market and butchery, as well as a bank, and a church. Although it was small, wealth was abundant. Every aspect of the town was synonymous: lovely buildings, costly goods, and exquisite taste.

As they approached their home, observing its grey marble coat, blue and silver spires that stabbed into the sky, and a garden of delphiniums, Gabriel furrowed his eyebrows as he couldn't help but feel overwhelmed. He wondered how the transition from event to event in his life had led to this exact moment, where he moved away from Fiddlefield—an average town with no distinct knowledge of its extraordinary existence—to a neighborhood armored in elitism and a supposed success. It fueled his anxieties and inner pressures that he knew would build up and implode within himself eventually. His prior memories seemed like a blur leading to his arrival; the conception being just a supercut of small, insignificant visions of his entire life. He saw some frames of his everyday schedule in Fiddlefield, the choirs he used to attend every Easter, and Fiddlefield's natural forest, where he would

4

write letters to himself about his life and his dreams of being a writer and what he hoped he would look and feel like one day. He was always told that there was a large difference between existing and living, that there was nothing worth existing for if you aren't indeed living it. Quintbridge was a hindrance to his *living*, and Gabriel entered this place expecting existence to therefore be impaired. He had already blocked any potential for a good experience, and he hadn't step foot outside yet.

Gabriel, as well as his younger sister, Cassandra, and his mother, Ms. Shabah, had pulled into the driveway of their future house. They sauntered inside, curiously inspecting each corner, frame, and ridge that lined the house's walls. It seemed just as large as the rest of the houses nearby. However, the rooms inside were accentuated by all the doors that reached the top of the ceiling, as if some group of giants had lived there before them.

"This house seems so cold. Where is the wood? It looks like it will be half a degree in the winter and more blazing than the Gobi in the summer. Or perhaps it will be more like the Egyptian deserts—I would like that much more. I remember reading about them when the tutors gave me a lesson on the history of Cleopatra and Marc Antony, and I found it fascinating," he stated from the grand entrance.

"Well, I quite like it. I think it makes the perfect home, and I bet you that the bedrooms are as ginormous as ballrooms, and I think the tutors and maids will enjoy this place too. I am so terribly excited to look through this place! Oh, I cannot wait!" responded Cassandra from above.

Squeals echoed throughout the home as Cassandra raced upstairs to see the rooms. She fell deeply in love with the room particularly above the garage, where there exists a window to look out at the neighbor's house to the left, another window to see the road and a few houses across the street, and another to see the backyard. A beautiful lawn lay ahead in the backyard before it extended to the edge of their property, fading into erosion, which Cassandra decided was ugly. Ms. Shabah also seemed to love this house, commenting on the fine development and furnishings as they explored. Gabriel thought it was suitable—not necessarily pleasant. A pessimism plagued the boy, but everyone was already so adjusted that his thoughts had no effect.

Although the room was empty, Ms. Shabah particularly adored the lovely study, explaining to the children how it would be perfect for language lessons, as well as a suitable place for the tutors to work throughout the upcoming school year. "A splendid home and quite the opportunity nestled within!" pronounced Ms. Shabah. It was always important to Ms. Shabah that her children were well-educated. She did not want to support them financially for the rest of their lives, so she made it her personal mission to make them eligible for success.

They settled in the kitchen for the rest of the day, unpacking their belongings, discussing their future lives, and arguing with Gabriel before being interrupted by a soft five knocks on their front door. A girl had appeared, looking barely older than Cassandra but younger than Gabriel, and she held a small gift basket with homemade candies and cakes scattered within. It was surrounded by pink and red decorations but was unevenly distributed along the sides. The basket so that it seemed cheap, but the girl had made it herself—the messiness intending to project character and personality. Gabriel and Cassandra opened the door, saw the basket, and did not think it to be personable whatsoever. It did look rather cheap.

"Hello, mister, good day miss. Welcome to Quintbridge, we are so extremely happy to have you here! The old neighbors were honestly too boring for the livelihood of this place. I mean, the annual hopscotch competition, which is coming up in the next few months, is something that everyone does, and if you aren't competing, it's still a custom that you watch, and they didn't even bother to come out and watch. Isn't that just frustrating? I may be rambling now—am I rambling? Terribly sorry if I am. Anyways, what are your names? It's so nice to meet you both!" said the girl.

Both Gabriel and Cassandra were flustered, feeling as if a hurricane of words had attacked them. They quickly exchanged glances at each other, understanding that they had both experienced the same thing—a flurry of a girl who spewed words out like she was over-flowing. They did hear the quick stepping of their mother from behind, seeming so eager to meet the new neighbor that had gone out of their way to introduce themselves. Gabriel began to answer her question.

"Hello, my name is Gabriel Shabah. This is my sister Cassandra, also nice to meet you—"

"What a coincidence! My name is also Cassandra! Cassandra Farrow. I feel like this is going to get a little bit confusing, you know, since we are both named Cassandra, so we are going to have to come up with some sort of nickname for each other. I feel like maybe I can stick with Cassandra, and you can adopt Cassie? Or maybe Cass is better. This is so interesting to me; I have never met another Cassandra before.

6

We are going to be the *best* of friends," she said with a large amount of enthusiasm.

Before Cassandra Shabah had the opportunity to respond to the girl, Cassandra Farrow noticed an older face that had appeared behind them. Knowing it was their mother, she smiled widely, flaunting her straight, white teeth in hopes of seeking an approval of the woman. The mother, Ms. Shabah, peered at the girl from the door with a returning smile, filled with her thoughts of adoration and intrigue for the girl. She decided to take control of the conversation and began to speak over her daughter.

"Good day, Cassandra. I'm Ms. Shabah, so nice to meet you. Please, could you tell me which house you come from? I'm only asking in order to know who I have met here and who I still need to meet. What a gorgeous girl you are!" she chuckled.

"Oh, of course, and thank you. I am actually from the house directly across the street. Do you see?" said Cassandra, pointing directly towards the house parallel to their house and the road.

"Ah. Yes. How beautiful your land is! Could you remind me of your full name once again?"

"Yes, ma'am. Cassandra Farrow." There was a sound of understanding, an '*Ah,*' followed by a long pause of silence before Cassandra Farrow continued. "Well, it was so nice to meet you all again. I'm a knock away if you need anything, and if you need someone to help introduce you to everyone, I am free to do so. Good day," she said before leaving the basket on the side of the front steps and prancing back toward her house—her dress flowing from her skips and the cool breeze in the air. Once Ms. Shabah had taken in the basket, delighted at the scent of the cakes and the candies inside, a plethora of confusion ensued. Cassandra and Gabriel emitted comments complaining about the kindness of the girl in a fashion that seemed arrogant and rude.

"She actually asked me to change my name! Who does that? I haven't met a person who, in the first instance of meeting them, asked me to change my name to something as bizarre as 'Cassie,'" Cassandra said.

"And I cannot believe she talked almost all of the time that we had met and cut me off in the middle of my greeting. Honestly strange," Gabriel interjected.

"Oh, please, be quiet! She was a courageous girl to even walk up the steps to people she has never met. She did not flaunt or complain or insult, so keep your mouth shut. I do not want to hear my children act as spoiled as two-week-old milk. To be frank, Cassie is a beautiful name to be used as a nickname, which is what she had meant in the first place. She was also incredibly kind talking with you, Gabriel, which we all know can be hard. Not only that, but she left a basket of homemade cakes. I am betting that you both don't know how to even whisk. To think that my children are containing the energy of an angry princess who cannot accept anything because it is unworthy is more than disappointing. I suggest not opening your mouth for the rest of the night about her in a negative manner. How dare you both!" yelled Ms. Shabah, scrutinizing their terrible behavior. The children did not talk any further. Cassandra especially felt upset at her mother yelling at her, feeling as if she hadn't done anything wrong.

The single thing that Ms. Shabah hated more than anything in the universe was a gossiper. She felt as if her kid's becoming gossipers was more detrimental to their lives than paralysis. She felt as if conditions such as paralysis can only slow down success and greatness but can never completely hinder it—leading to only nothing but the immovable body that cannot achieve anything. However, something as catastrophic as a reputation dictated by gossip and whispers is more damaging than anything else. She talked to great lengths about the comparison between paralysis and something else, specifically because that is her biggest irrational fear—paralysis of the entire body. Ms. Shabah consistently called out her children for whispering like gossips do but was now more afraid of them turning into gossips after adjusting to their life in Quintbridge. The land of the rich was sure to influence children into a forced facade, where they must keep up a persona and chat about people to make themselves seem better, just like the rest of the people do. It all seemed too disgraceful for Ms. Shabah to think about, so she decided to close her eyes. She was too proud to even think of her family in a negative light.

Gabriel took out his diary once again, and put in another entry, the second in one day, in deep black ink from a pen he found inside the house:

"What a day I have had. I have met one of the girls here—our neighbor across the street—and I am confused. She talked sporadically and wouldn't let us finish our sentences. I wonder what the rest of the neighborhood would be like—would they all act the same? I hope not, for that was a terrible and humiliating introduction. Mother complained about Cassandra and I's thoughts, but we were speaking in all honesty. If I were to publish this diary, would the public react the same way my mother did? Are my thoughts as terrible as she describes? I will detract them if other people agree with my mother. My first sleep in this dark neighborhood awaits. Quintbridge is the name—what a beautiful name."

This would be his last journal entry for a long while. He had finished his last page of his current journal and he would not receive another journal for some time. He felt like he was the only boy in the world who would keep a journal, but that did not stop him from tracking the events in his life. The tracking of his life wasn't the only thing he did, however. Surprisingly, he wrote many pages about his love for the dolphin.

He mostly wrote about the beauty of a dolphin, how it sailed through the waters of the world and whistled amongst themselves. It was an intelligent creature that represented everything he wished for in life. Although they could not technically breath underwater, Gabriel considered them able to breathe because they could stay underwater all that time. He thought it was a superpower. If Gabriel were a dolphin, he would simply jump through the waters, entertaining everything that he came across and eating all the fish he could catch without a worry in the world. In the future, he simply would not have time for journaling, and the grip of Quintbridge would hold him with tremendous strength. It would be his last entry for a while.

CHAPTER II

Later in the week, Ms. Shabah had become inspired. Considering the brave actions of Cassandra Farrow for being the first person to introduce themselves to them, let alone the fact that she did so without waiting for the Shabah family to come to her, Ms. Shabah wondered if her children were to do the same or just wait. Wanting to implement some beginning to this upcoming life here, Ms. Shabah ordered them to ask Cassandra Farrow to reveal everything there is to know about Quintbridge and its residents, but obviously in the historical sense. Gabriel and Cassandra both walked out of the house reluctantly, wishing that their neighbor would have been someone more relaxed and outgoing rather than interruptive. Unwillingly, they trudged through their yard and crossed the road towards the driveway of the Farrow household.

While approaching the household, the siblings noticed that the mother, Ms. Farrow, was watching them and their house through the window. It was an uncomfortable sight and made the two feel slightly uneasy to continue approaching. They stepped up to the front door, knocked a few times, and were immediately confronted with Ms. Farrow. Her figure was more on the plumper side in comparison to their mother; her flabby arms were crossed, and her fingers dangled from the end that was tucked in her elbow, revealing black stains on the tips of them; her nature seemed judgmental and harrowing, deeply concerning the two siblings. Gabriel asked her if the "beautiful Cassandra" is available to walk around with, but Ms. Farrow shut him down. She mentioned a few things about how Cassandra is unable to be with children around the neighborhood because of some unfavorable conditions which she refused to elaborate on.

Upsettingly, Gabriel and Cassandra walked back down the Farrow household's driveway but were quickly surprised by the appearance of Cassandra Farrow. She briefly mentioned how she snuck outside once she saw them, going through the window so ever silently, and had crawled through the bottom of the house where the crawlspace is. She then climbed out of a small opening the size of a large dog, which was made after a water accident had broken pieces of the wood guarding the tank, and weathering had taken its course. After brushing dirt off herself, she looked up at the two with glee and quickly ran over to ask them why they were at her home.

"Hello, you two. What brings you by? Also, my mother does *not* want you two and me hanging out, which is why I had to make a fool of myself by crawling, and with that, I apologize. But, back to the question, why are Gabriel Shabah and Cassie Shabah standing at my front door?" she asked. Cassandra Shabah rolled her eyes at the sound of her new nickname being spoken by Cassandra Farrow.

"We are here because we wanted to ask if you could possibly give us a tour of the neighborhood. We are deeply interested in meeting the rest of the residents here and have found that your cheerful company will make the perfect guide for both of us. You also seem exceedingly knowledgeable about this neighborhood, and we wouldn't ask anyone else for information," said Gabriel, lying. Cassandra Shabah forced a large smile, attempting to prove that they were truly eager to receive a tour when, in actuality, she resented her. Gabriel felt guilty about lying to her but did not want to make his sister feel alone in her hatred.

"Of course, I would be delighted," said Cassandra Farrow. "However, I do see it fit that Cassandra needs a sort of nickname; introductions will be quite confusing without one. I can tell she does not believe that Cassie is a mature choice for one—I did see her roll her eyes—but I still believe a nickname necessary. Do you have any suggestions?" Cassandra Shabah blushed in embarrassment about what the girl said, but replied in her ever-sarcastic voice.

"I guess—if it *is* such a necessity—you may call me Andra. I have thought it over back at my place and consider it the best possible option out of all others."

"Splendid! I shall introduce you immediately. However, let's quickly hurry through this shortcut through the front yards here—it will be quicker!" Cassandra bolted towards her next-door neighbor's yard. Gabriel and Andra both followed her, a smile of surprise appearing on Gabriel's face, while a frenzied expression was stuck on Andra's.

Gabriel and Andra both thought it to be peculiar that Cassandra did not want to walk down the rest of the driveway and take the road immediately. They did not question it, though, because they had already found her to be quite the eccentric girl. After cutting through the next-door neighbor's yard, they moved back down to the road slowing their movement down to a leisurely pace. As the birds chirped through the

11

silence of the neighborhood and the housecats made journeys in-between and around houses, Cassandra commented on the dynamic of the neighborhood, and how its fame has contributed far more than the majority of its actual residents. She talked about how once people learn where someone comes from, it changes their initial idea of them and places a rigid frame around their existence. Quintbridge is that initial frame but made of steel and plated with gold. It is the luck of some selective past residents who happened to be successful in one field or another that contributed to this frame.

There was once a man who struck it lucky with gold, and he chose to build his first house here. Then, his brother-in-law sold his printing press company, which gifted him with enough money to attain the ability to move to Quintbridge too. His buyers also enjoyed his personality so much that they decided on bringing their belongings to Quintbridge. Others also got lucky, selling a large piece of farmland that was virgin and hadn't had the gift of crops planted on it yet for a sum of money far too high than it should be, and others through intellectual ways like writing novels and gifted lawyers. A famous athlete, who competed alongside Romania on the wrestling team in the Olympic games, and won the gold medal, chose to take his future by the edge of the pond in the center of the neighborhood. Otherwise, if those people hadn't agreed on this place, the neighborhood would be nothing but a commonplace for people who needed somewhere to live—nothing pricy in the slightest. Her gold frame analogy was inspired by the acts of the first man to live here—the gold rusher—and seems to work with every case of a person in Quintbridge. Her well-thought analogy had surprised Andra and Gabriel and allowed them to take on some liking for her; Gabriel was especially impressed, raising his standards unlike his sister, who continued to be spellbound in her unfortunate resentment.

Cassandra was very intelligent. It was not something that was easily detected by someone—even her family did not know that she was very smart—but it was her personality that made it difficult for people to understand her in that way. She knew that she annoyed people by talking at great lengths, but she felt that she had so much to say and would be uncomfortable keeping it inside herself. Her intelligence was often hidden from the external, but she knew that she was smarter than most. More than half of the world's population believed that they were above-average intelligence, but Cassandra Farrow thought herself to be capable of not understanding just literature and mathematics, but also social interaction, ideas, and the supposed 'street smarts.' She was

12

constantly shamed, though, so she tried to keep everything locked away deep inside her.

The walk through the winding roads of Quintbridge seemed longer than they expected, exhausting the three as they walked up and down hills every few feet. Gabriel and Andra did not seem to notice the great extent to which the neighborhood is laid out but venturing through it first-hand had given them incredulous amounts of insight. It was large enough to fit just over a hundred families in each of their respective homes, and each plot of land could satisfy even the hungriest of landowners. The roads had eventually led the Shabah siblings and Cassandra to notice two small red-haired boys, about the age of eight, running in diagonals and circles, picking up rocks and sticks and throwing them in every direction, and running into the woods screaming something that seemed gibberish.

"Those two are the Lillis twins. Their parents are both Irish in the most stereotypical way possible, with the heavy accent and the red-hair-pale-skin combination and all. Their entire family is the same, except for the fact that those twins don't have an accent. If you ask me, I loathe those twins. They are completely erratic, annoying, and insane. Honestly troublemaking," Cassandra said.

The twins floated their way deep into the woods until their carrot-top hair blended with the background colors and their pale skin wasn't visible amongst the green leaves. The twins didn't seem to have a care in the world for anything except their mental adventures. It reminded Andra of a toddler who waddles around in search of a mysterious unicorn or runs from imaginary goblins. She thought the twins were rather cute than mischievous and thought Cassandra a small part jealous of the twins. After all, they indeed had freedom, and Cassandra seemed to have none of the sort, constantly locked in a house with her fearsome mother guarding the door. Freedom is not the ability to leave and go wherever in the world, but rather the ability to live carelessly among others, as whoever is free can do.

Cassandra then led the brother and sister to pass by the Ledger house close to the pond in the center, where a group of boys had huddled together. They were shouting encouragements to a young boy who had performed a trick on the curb of the road, using a slab of flat wood connected to four wheels and landing on a single foot. Excitedly, Cassandra, Gabriel, and Andra all ran over towards the crowd.

"Well, fancy seeing you guys here. These two are the new neighbors across from my house. Andra and Gabriel."

"Pleasure to meet you," said one of the boys, shaking their hands respectively.

"Yes, it is nice to meet you. We could use a fresh set in Quintbridge. It's hell in here, especially since everyone nowadays is so old and boring," said another.

Gabriel and Andra both turned to each other and smiled. A mutual appreciation for the normality of these boys was made, and simultaneously, they mentally agreed that these boys will have a larger impact on the friendships they make in the neighborhood. At least, they would make sure of it since they wanted nothing to do with Cassandra. "It's nice to meet you all. I see you have a little toy that you are riding around on—something of a board with wheels. We have never seen anything like it before," said Gabriel.

"We made it ourselves. We searched through a magazine that we found on the ground outside of the market, and we noticed this interesting machine called a scooter. We tried making a scooter, but it was too hard to have only two wheels, so we added two more. We also don't need a handle—it's more fun that way."

"Would you teach us some tricks like we just witnessed?"

The boys were all surprised by the eagerness of the boy and his sister, for Cassandra Farrow had never wanted to try riding their invention. The eldest three boys grabbed Gabriel by the arm and took him to the side, gifting him with their 'beginners board' as they called it. All the boys jutted in advice on what to do, a myriad of tricks he could perform, and cheered for him to get on immediately. Gabriel was nervous but seemed to get rid of all fear once he attempted to ride the board. As he did so, he wobbled, and almost fell over. It seemed quite embarrassing to Gabriel, but the other boys were respectful and held at his waist and shoulders to keep his balance. Gabriel felt equally comfortable with the boys here as he did with Cassandra but still longed to continue talking to the vivacious girl more than attempting to ride the curious invention with the boys. He could not understand why he felt the need to continue talking to her, since it was clear his sister did not like her. Cassandra was all he could think about. Gabriel stepped on the board but was thrust ahead by one of the boys who had given him a small shove, rolling him onto the daunting flat road at what seemed a stupendous speed—only five miles an hour. He cried as he rolled away, but then started feeling overwhelmed with surprise that he hadn't fallen yet, because all the boys had let go, not to his knowledge. They cheered when he successfully rode across the pavement. Gabriel laughed in

14

amazement at his actions, and ran back towards the boys, jumping like a stimulated. They started jumping together, and Cassandra laughed at their ridiculousness.

Andra and another boy in the crowd had decided to take it much slower, separating themselves to practice on their own. The boy had chosen the longest board they had to ride and asked Andra to join him for the first ride rather than going alone. He regarded the practice of going alone as barbaric, stating that it is more effective to learn collaboratively than to learn alone, straight into the deep end of the water. Andra was impressed with his clever logic. However, she wanted to appear indifferent to him and made a fuss about having to ride the board with someone else, but the boy was successful in persuading her that it was necessary. She reluctantly agreed, and they went on a small ride around the route of the Ledger's semicircular driveway, accelerating Andra's heartbeat when the boy placed his hands by her hips. He unexpectedly broke into conversation.

"I must admit to you—although I seem like it, I am not even a Ledger. An upsetting confession, I know. I'm Jason, the boy who lives in the house directly to the left of yours. I solely hang around with these kids 'cause they are more fun than sitting at home reading with my mother," said he.

"I could tell," Andra retorted. "You weren't as crazy as the other boys were when my brother didn't break his ankle from that board. Your reaction was bland. Blatantly bland."

"Ah, so it must be easy to tell. Perhaps I should change my attitude and begin screaming at the sight of someone *not* being injured?"

"No, absolutely not. I think you are perfectly suitable the way you are right now. Keep it this way, I do not want a façade separating us."

"I was only joking. I would never do such a thing. How forward of you to think that I would change that quickly!" Jason replied. Andra laughed at his sarcasm and seemed to hold her smile for the next few seconds as they enjoyed a comfortable silence. "If you lean, it turns. I don't know how they made it this way, but it is better to just lean instead of readjusting your position each time you need to turn."

They continued to ride down the path ahead slowly and he guided her sways to turn left and right, meandering around the road. Andra cherished the trip, considering this new mysterious boy as a lovely face. He contained each of the perfect qualities she particularly observed: a chiseled face like the statues created during the Greek times,

15

balanced introversion and extroversion within himself, and a fantastic sense of humor like that of Herman Melville. She could only wonder about possible scenarios with him for a short while because soon, they arrived back at the crowd of boys, and engaged in a conversation about how Andra was "undeniably legendary" at riding for her first time, and how Jason is "such an incredible teacher," all of which made them blush in compliments. The boys decided it would be best to showcase their skills like they are performing in a play. The two agreed and began whispering to each other quickly. A burst of giggles soon followed like small children learning a secret, and the boys were instructed to be seated as they perform a show. Andra picked up her board and ran behind a large tree, hiding from the view of the boys. However, her laughter caused her body to continuously shake, obscuring her hide and making herself visible. The whole thing seemed utterly foolish.

"Ladies, ladies, it is time for the main event," Jason said as he strode towards them, "It is time for our Missus to speed faster than lightning by a slab of wood. We invite you all to watch as she breaks the world record for the fastest person alive!"

The audience was starting to laugh but was quickly interrupted by a sudden movement. Andra bolted towards the road, laughing hysterically as she ran; the ruffles of her clothes breezing in the wind and her hair moving in such a way like a serene wash of a wave on a sandy beach. She hurled towards a curb separating a small strip of grass and the smoothly paved road. She threw the board towards the grass, the board rolling its way speedily over the shrubs and past the concrete curb, where it moved in a consistent motion on the polished road. Andra attempted to place one of her feet on top of the board, but by doing so, she launched the board further than anticipated, lunging forward quickly. However, she had accidentally caught her other foot in a small crack between the earth and the curb causing her to fall backward onto the ground; a loud crack emerged from the bottom of her ankle. Gabriel shot up from his seat with the other boys, mouth agape and greatly concerned. Andra screamed in excruciating pain while she sat back up and observed that her ankle had moved much farther than its maximum potential, and was pointing in its opposite direction. A deep purple color flooded her pale skin, causing great concern among the boys. Her bone stuck out, gushing blood down her foot and onto the ground. Cassandra and Gabriel grabbed her up onto her foot and hobbled their way back towards their house.

CHAPTER III

Ms. Shabah watched her children leave with the kind Cassandra Farrow, and then made her way through the house, cleaning and brushing up pieces of furniture and washing the countertops of each table. She began to hear some shrieks coming from outside. Ms. Shabah moved toward the window to peer out into the neighborhood where she saw small groups of individuals gathered around their respective mailboxes. They held small letters and were reading the contents intently, a gasp arising from the content. Confused but simultaneously curious, she decided to go to the front of her house and check to see if there was any mail for her. She walked up her driveway and noticed that the crowds of people were looking at her, watching her walk with faces of sadness or longing, or hatred. She was confused by this large variety and seemed more confused that seemingly everyone was staring at her. Ms. Shabah checked her mailbox but seemed to find nothing.

She scanned the area around the mailbox in the case that it accidentally dropped, but still found nothing. She turned around, looking at everyone who was holding these letters, and she heard the loud whispering of her name being repeated in each group. Ms. Shabah was about to leave when she heard an old woman walking behind her with a small piece of paper poking out from the pocket of her brown fur coat. The lady was walking three small dogs who could not be properly controlled and were dragging her about the roads. It seemed a ridiculous sight as she watched the old lady of far greater size than the small dogs be handled around by their enthusiasm to walk around. But very quickly she resumed her initial interest, which was seeing what information this letter held, and so she slowly walked up to the old woman and asked her, in the kindest manners she could elicit, if she carried a copy of the letter that everyone was reading. The woman paused for a moment, staring directly at Ms. Shabah in disbelief, as if she needed to determine if she was completely serious or joking, but then reached into her pocket, reaffirming the theory that the paper was indeed the letter. Ms. Shabah tried to take the letter, but the old lady held some strange force on it as if she did not want Ms. Shabah to take the letter, but she eventually acquiesced. Ms. Shabah held the letter close to her face and read it entirely.

Dearest Neighbors,

JUNE 7, 1900. I hope everyone has had a fantastic week so far. My children and I are going to do a small cleanup of the neighborhood in its entirety on the weekends—we found a sufficient amount of trash nearby so we decided that it would be best to begin cleaning. I am sure you are all aware that we have new arrivals here in Quintbridge! It is quite a shame, however, that the bashful new neighbors, that have recently made their home within this established neighborhood, have stripped the blue house entirely from being bought by someone different. They seem to not know the true ways of the neighborhood, unrealizing in the fact that their beautiful home has been sought after by members of this neighborhood, not excluding myself, for what seems like a millennium. I am truly depressed to see that the blue house—shining with marble and attractive delphiniums—will soon rot into a dumpster since no one but myself and perhaps a few others know how to manage an estate like that properly. These clueless neighbors will see what it takes to be a resident here, and how you must truly have earned your spot. Some of us deserve that house, others, not so much. I wish blessings upon you all and cheers to the new neighbors who will slowly turn this establishment into a shantytown for the homeless to shoot heroin.

Carol Farrow

Ms. Shabah completed reading the letter and paused for a moment—looking deeply ahead of her while her brain generated some thoughts about what she had just seen: a disgrace. She reread it, and then once more, and a final time, until her grip seemed to crinkle the delicate paper in a fit of distress. She threw it to her side and loudly grunted, like she was exhaling angrily and gritting her teeth, before turning back to the old woman. She shook her head in silence—the only noise being the crowds of people discussing the content of the letter and the breeze of the wind rustling the leaves in the canopy overhead—and then gave the letter back with a curtsey, thanking her for her exceeding levels of kindness.

"I told you honey; I wanted to make sure you understood what you were reading—the devil's thoughts!" said the kind old woman.

Ms. Shabah had loosened herself, rolling out her shoulders and twisting her neck to both sides before expelling her inner thoughts into the air. "How dare she slander me like this! First, she insulted my family to the greatest extent and then proceeded to offend my house, which she seems so eager to attain herself that her jealousy is practically bleeding from these pages. My house is mine in the most respective and deserving way. I am in complete disbelief that a putrid woman like this Carol Farrow—whose child I had just met earlier this week—is sending terrifyingly terrible letters around, and no one is doing anything except reading and shrieking and laughing. She cannot go around saying total lies and rude, inappropriate things about my family, my deserved home, and myself…. Oh, I am going to have a word with her, most definitely!"

"Honey, I wouldn't even bother. She is not only as wicked as a witch but as ruthless as the devil himself! My suggestion is to simply walk it out. Join me?"

"Absolutely. May I get your name? You have been beyond kind."

"Yes, dear. I am Hadiza Kabila, a resident of this neighborhood for over twenty years. Only until a few years ago, when I met that godawful Carol over there did I unknowingly subscribe to her disgusting mail. The drama-seekers here love it, though, and she seems to have developed a fanbase. The sole reason by which they love reading her letters is that they simply have nothing more interesting in their own miserable lives. I don't know why she writes letters and complaints and decides to distribute them, but that is what she does and has always done. I never thought that one day they will be about someone in particular since she has never actually called anyone out by name or reference, but rather she calls out actions. I find it completely strange that she did that—and with no hesitation! She sent the letter to practically everyone. When I saw you walking up to your mailbox, I just knew you would ask me. I actually slowed down, in hopes you would ask me and not some crazy neighbor who is siding with the woman. Thank God you did, but I am sorry for you."

"How gross! Thank you for your kindness, Ms. Kabila. It is truly appreciated. I think I needed to see that letter."

"You most certainly did. It was atrocious, and now you know who to avoid. Everyone who has been at the short end of the stick from these letters are genuinely beautiful human beings once you get to know them. Haven't you only moved here not even a few days?"

"Yes, exactly. I moved here two days ago. How concerning is it that her youngest daughter, who I sent to walk with my children, came over to give us a basket of treats? Why would she allow that, but then write a ludicrous letter?"

"The woman is crazed," said Ms. Kabila, rolling her eyes.

"Honestly! After reading it, I feel like, perhaps, she just wants to be a journalist of some sort, or recount every existing thought and experience that she ever had and put it in writing form for everyone to read. She is acting like she is a figure of wonder: someone who thinks they are above all—like a president or a royal."

"The good thing is that no one would want to read her complaints, anyways. Trust me, I am completely on your side."

"Thank you. How dare she? How *dare* she?" muttered Ms. Shabah.

"Well, anyway, how has your adjustment to the neighborhood been? I know that the events that just happened probably made this adjustment stranger, but if we disregard it, have your family moved in well?"

"Splendid, otherwise. My home has come together quite nicely. Where on this long road do you live?"

"I live near the entrance, the closest house to the pond. Right before I left for my walk, which I do daily, I saw your children and the Farrow girl walking around—"

"Oh goodness! I better get them away from her. I do not want any attachments to that terrible family, or more so that terrible woman."

"Ms. Shabah, relax your nerves! They are perfectly in good hands. The Farrow girl is unlike the rest of her family. Her brother and sisters are all biological to the mother and father, but not that girl, however. She was adopted. Seems sad because they don't like her much. I find her lovely. Sometimes she sneaks out for some early-morning tea with me, and we chat about the political climates and worldly affairs, she even talks to me about the things I like, such as my dogs or my fur coats. She is incredibly mature for only fifteen."

"Well, that is wonderful that she does that sort of thing! I'm not remotely surprised about her hardships with her family because she isn't biological; I personally knew a large number of people who were adopted, and they turned out neglected and abused by their families. They seem like a terrible bunch to be raising such a kind girl, and how she got to this level of kindness is astounding."

"I agree. However, Cassandra is the fruition of all good—the very little that there is— in that family," said Ms. Kabila, as she walked carefully with her small dog and her large cane. It was made of wood with special engravings that seemed of tradition, which Ms. Shabah deeply admired.

While they made their loop around the neighborhood, Ms. Shabah had taken a strong liking to the graceful and courteous Ms. Kabila. She had advice that had never been given to her by anyone else, and she felt like she was *cared for* by a member of her new community. After they made a complete loop, Ms. Shabah was extremely tired and decided to go back inside to rest and get some water, mentioning that it felt like she had just taken an hour hike and she is incredibly parched. Ms. Kabila laughed and decided to continue with another few laps. As she walked inside, she could hear a faint argument taking place a few hundred yards away.

In the middle of the road, the neighbors directly next door to Ms. Shabah's house, the Victoriana household, had been yelling at Carol Farrow; their argument was booming throughout the vicinity, yet nothing was comprehensible. Ms. Shabah wanted to derive the exact behavior that Carol Farrow was adopting and hid behind the small wall on the side of the garage—the echo of their conversation amplified by the hollow garage that Ms. Shabah was standing in. The lady Victoriana had been sobbing profusely, and tears streamed down her face. Her husband stood next to her—a solemn expression on his face, his smile still as clearwater. He stared towards the abyss, looking at nothing rather than something. Ms. Shabah imagined that while he stared, the noise of his wife and Carol Farrow were bouncing through his ear canals and leaving as they pleased, making no real sounds but purely noise. Carol

Farrow stood proudly, smirking occasionally as she yelled back at the Victoriana couple. Carol Farrow's bright-colored sweater of pink and green stripes seemed to contradict her unappealing nature, where instead of being a bright charisma among the world of shadows, she was truly what cast the shadow. After a minute of intense focus, some of the conversations could be heard:

"Ms. Farrow, I am not even sure—how you found out—about our situation, but it is truly—none of your business—to spread! —You are appropriating an image about us—an image that is damaging!"

"You act like your façade about your own life isn't damaging enough. I have had enough of your lies and fake persona. Priding yourself on being 'the richest among us' is not only disgusting, but also embarrassing."

"Leave us—alone!" Lady Victoriana said, intermittently sobbing in between phrases.

"No! It is my responsibility to—"

"Stop! It is not your responsibility!" interrupted Sir Victoriana. Lady Victoriana continued, "None of our personal affairs have anything to do with you. It is purely our responsibility, not yours. You have become some disgusting human being—what even are you anymore?"

"You act like I have *become* disgusting, but was I truly? Or have I always been like this? You knew of what I do before you had told me this information; complaining about your situation to me as if I am going to stay put and let this go by."

Soon, Lady Victoriana shook her head in disgust, letting out a frustrated exhale as she cried. They dispersed, the Victorianas going back towards their household, where a large slam emerged from their front door. Ms. Shabah observed that Carol Farrow was still standing on her driveway, shaking her head with a disgusted, egotistical look while her arms crossed and foot tapped. Although Ms. Shabah was quite confused about what exactly was happening, she seemed to understand that Carol had developed a reputation for her intrusive and malevolent conduct, which seemed to be recognized by the rest of the neighborhood. She began to loathe the evil Carol Farrow, who seemed to have a grip over the people here, unknowingly believing she has gained respect rather than discomfort and detestation. Ms. Shabah decided that since she hasn't met most of the other neighbors, she should make herself their acquaintance before Carol Farrow's letters influence the idea of her. Instead of approaching the Victoriana household first, she chose the opposite direction, where the Grealm household was.

Immediately, she was on her way there for a chat, considering her appearance. She still glistened in sweat from her walk with the graceful Ms. Kabila, so she decided to maintain her authenticity by remaining as candid as possible, hoping to have the idea that meeting the neighbor next door was a thought instantaneously popping within her mind.

She knocked only once before a petite and stubby lady speedily opened the door, as if she had been waiting for her by the window and perfectly timed when she would knock. The lady seemed about thirty years old, but she couldn't tell. Her skin revealed one age while her facial structure revealed another, causing a weird combination that made her age seem enigmatic. It deeply disoriented Ms. Shabah.

"Hello, dear. Can I do something for you?" said the woman in a bothered tone.

"Yes, are you Ms. Grealm? I just moved in next door, and I thought I should introduce myself."

"Oh, yes, my apologies. Would you come inside? Wine? I have red, white, and any other kind that someone would ask for," said the woman. "The name's Bonnie by the way. I don't usually talk to people here, but you seem like a particularly interesting neighbor, and quite the pretty one."

Ms. Shabah accepted her compliment and followed her as she talked nonsense about her dated flooring and artwork lining her yellow walls. She led them both to a glass cellar filled with hundreds of full bottles of wine, entirely astounding Ms. Shabah. It was at least twenty feet across and shaped like a cube, filled with wine from a variety of decades ranging back to the early 1800s, worth more than her house itself. Bonnie jumped onto a ladder, reaching for a particular bottle about two feet above her. Afterward, she poured two full glasses of wine. Ms. Shabah expected the woman to give her one of the glasses, but she just gave the rest of the bottle to her. The bottle had less than a quarter left in it, which was less than half of a glass that she poured. Ms. Shabah thought the lady an oddity—stranger than anyone she could have imagined. They both took a seat on the emerald sofas inside the cellar and left the door wide open.

"So, I am aware that me popping in here is a little extraordinary," said Ms. Shabah, "But I was hoping you could help me with understanding something. You seem quite observant so let me know if this rings a bell for you. Just a moment ago, as I was finishing a walk, I noticed that Ms. Farrow was arguing with the Victoriana couple. Do you know what this is all about?" Ms. Shabah felt ill as she asked that question, believing that she sounded like a young girl desperate for a juicy piece of information.

"Oh, yes, did you not hear? They just went broke, and Carol wrote another one of her stupid letters informing everyone. I found it quite ridiculous, but she is the news of the neighborhood. A secret cannot truly be kept in the presence of a truth-seeker. Carol is just the best mode of truth that we have because she gives it all. If you can navigate through her opinions and her tone, it does provide useful information," said Bonnie.

"But how do you know she is telling the truth? Have you not for a moment thought that she is entirely disgusting in her behavior? I mean, she wrote letters about me and my family, completely out of a vendetta she has against us. The crazy part is that we haven't even met her."

"Yes, dear, I suppose you are correct—" says Bonnie, who is cut off from her sentence by her young son barging through the door. He anxiously paced throughout the house, ignoring calls from his mother. The small sediments on his shoes also spread along a newly cleaned carpet, making Ms. Grealm incredibly upset.

"I see you have met my son. His name is Jason, normally kind and pleasant, but I can't help feeling like he is distressed."

"Ah, I see. Yes, he does look quite distressed. Should we ask what he is rummaging for?"

"No ma'am, I don't think so. He will be adequate in a moment. He's a fencer for the county, and he wants to try out for the Olympic team! Isn't that splendid?"

"Quite! I am jealous that he has found his passions quite early in life. I wonder how he will be pursuing them in a few years," said Ms. Shabah with complete adoration.

"Oh, his passions do not lie within the foil, but rather within the piano. I bought him a grand one in the room adjacent to my office, and I could not bear it any longer! His music is so terrible because of his lack of knowledge that he makes a bleeding noise that sounds like hell! I cannot bear it."

"Well, you may be happy to hear that Gabriel is fond of the piano and would be glad to teach him on my account. Also, my daughter Cassandra needs a sport to do in her life, and fencing would be wonderful for her. Maybe we could arrange a sort of trade between the children?"

"What a lovely idea! I believe that Jason would love that idea truly!"

24

Their conversation stopped abruptly when Jason ran across the house completely, holding a bandage. It greatly puzzled the pair of ladies sitting down, and they concentrated on his movements. When he opened the door, screeches of a young girl could be heard for a slight moment, before they were muffled by the door's closing. It took a small moment of silence and concentration before Ms. Shabah jumped back onto her feet, realizing that the screams were of her daughter. She excused herself, and hurried immediately out of the house, where Bonnie followed.

Ms. Grealm stood by the door, watching with her mouth agape. Cassandra Shabah's ankle was turned completely horizontal as she limped her way towards Ms. Shabah's house; a sight of blood and bone so grotesque that it made her feel nauseous. Ms. Shabah ran at a superhuman speed, catching up with her daughter and taking over the role of Cassandra Farrow, where she made haste towards her carriage to go immediately to the hospital. Neighbors gathered by the road, a few residents offering help that was ignored by the focused haze of motherly instinct. Ms. Shabah placed Cassandra in the back seat of her vehicle, sitting next to her brother and Jason Grealm. Cassandra attempted to join them as they journeyed to the emergency room, but her mother quickly called her back inside. Regrettably, Cassandra walked back towards her house, facing Andra as she watched her get into her carriage.

Cassandra Shabah's screams were louder than ever once the carriage began to move. Her face was covered in infinite tears, permanently stuck in an expression of pure agony. She was sandwiched between Jason and her brother, whose hands were stained in her blood. Ms. Shabah could do no more than continue to drive, recognizing and accepting that she will be giving an immense dose of pain to poor Cassandra Shabah. Once they arrived at the hospital, a horde of paramedics arrived at their carriage, carrying the girl inside on a stretcher. Ms. Shabah followed them; the boys attempted to as well but were ultimately unsuccessful as Ms. Shabah ordered them to stay where they once were. Once the doors of the hospital had closed, the sounds of Cassandra Shabah could no longer be heard. Gabriel and Jason sat down on the pavement outside of the vehicle, simply understanding and grasping what they had witnessed.

Gabriel felt frustrated at himself for not properly making sure that Cassandra would be secure and felt that his cautious nature had somehow turned off at this moment. He took complete accountability for what had happened—however, mentally, Jason felt at fault. His heart ached completely for her, as the image of her smile imprinted in his mind. He felt that his detrimental disadvantage of being selfish for public appeasement had bled through in this experience and caused a total consequence. His soul felt as if it had been torn in half when Andra was wheeled inside because he had come up with this idea and possibly ruined her future of walking.

CHAPTER IV

The next morning, after the paramount surgery had taken place and Cassandra had begun to awake from her sleepy slumber, Gabriel and Ms. Shabah stared curiously at her. The girl's eyes fluttered like butterfly wings, stinging from the absence of tears. Her mouth creased into a tired yawn, before transforming into a lovely smile that revealed her perfectly straight and white teeth.

Once they realized that Andra had awoken, they cheered in excitement, which brightened Cassandra's mood momentarily, before she felt a small pain in her ankle and realized what had happened. Her drowsiness mixed with her feelings of regret had made her switch into a dull mood, where she laid her head back down on the soft hospital pillows, exhaling.

"Not to worry, Cassandra! You will be healed in no time! The doctor said that incidents such as these are extremely common and easy to heal as long as you don't move," said Ms. Shabah to her sweet daughter, sensing that she feels let down by the catastrophe.

"I know mother. I just don't understand how that even happened. I had trembled many times in life before this, and I had never broken any sort of bone—it is broken, right?" Cassandra questioned.

"Yes, darling, it is broken."

"It's just bad luck, that's all!" remarked Gabriel.

"Shut up Gabriel! I do not care for your snarking."

"I am just saying—"

"Well, don't! If you had actually looked after me instead of laughing at my attempt, then this wouldn't have happened."

"Well excuse me, but you offered to ride it! I thought, by the basis of your level of confidence, that you had known how to properly ride it!"

"Children!" interrupted Ms. Shabah, "Do not have an argument at this time! Cassandra, there is nothing that Gabriel could have done differently, it is bad luck. Gabriel, enough snarking! We have had enough of your jokes!"

"Sorry! I am just saying!" answered Gabriel frustratedly. "Maybe this is the reason I am pessimistic, because of your treatment of me! In fact, this entire argument is completely unnecessary. I enjoy my life, and you make me feel guilty about it!"

The discussion halted when the doctors had walked back into the room, getting ready to hand out the mandatory paperwork to discharge the young girl. Her fit, rooted in deep regret of her actions, had caused an outburst that angered Gabriel. Cassandra was handed some crutches to walk on and was quickly out of the building.

The drive home was awkward, as it seemed that each of them had a reason to be mad at the other. Gabriel broke the silence:

"Honestly, you should have broken your entire leg so badly that you couldn't have walked. It would be better anyway, considering how furiously you annoy me."

"Gabriel! How dare you! Don't speak in such words, ever!" replied Ms. Shabah.

Cassandra was flustered at the comment and furrowed her eyebrows in deep anger. Whenever she did such a thing, she would remain quiet until spoken to, to which she would always reply aggressively. Like an animal, her standoffish attitude was untamed and continued to be so, until eventually she was left alone to contemplate. Soon, they had arrived back home, where Cassandra Farrow was waiting on the side of their driveway, curled into a ball like she was extremely cold. When the doors had opened and the three Shabahs walked out, Cassandra Farrow ran down the driveway, hollering and holding another slip of paper. She immediately ran past the two children and handed it to Ms. Shabah, stating that it was from her mother. The note read as follows:

Dearest Neighbors,

JUNE 17, 1900. The cleanup was a success! I have never loved the state of this neighborhood more than ever before. Well, that is for the most part. There is still one family that cannot seem to get a grasp on their lives here and this is making it exceptionally difficult for the rest of us. Don't you seem to find it particularly uncanny and ever so strange that the newcomers, the Shabah family, had been making a screaming noise for hours on end? I truly believe that this distraction is completely unnecessary, furthering my point that they shouldn't live here. Is there anyone that couldn't hear that young girl screeching like she was dying? Immature, honestly.

Carol Farrow

Ms. Shabah had read it aloud, causing the two young children to shriek in shock. They felt what they just read was beyond disgraceful. Cassandra Farrow stood beside them in a slight embarrassment, where she grabbed her elbow with her other arm and looked down, twisting her ankles side to side. She demanded her children go inside and stay there, and ordered Cassandra Farrow to go back home, but do so carefully to not be caught sneaking by her mother.

Then, in what seemed like a rush, Ms. Shabah made her way to the front door of the Farrow household. On her way up her driveway, she had purposefully squashed a fresh orange tulip that had grown by the stairs, expressing her intense irritation with Carol Farrow.

Four strong knocks slammed at the Farrow Household's front door. Carol Farrow opened the door, puzzled at who it could be, but her face soon dropped when she noticed it was the Shabah mother.

"What do you want?" she asked Ms. Shabah.

"What do I want? What do *you* want? I have done nothing to you, and this is the second letter you have written about me. Not to me. About me," said Ms. Shabah in a raised voice, holding her letter in her hand.

"Who gave that to you? That isn't for you."

"Well, clearly it has my name smeared all over it so I assume it is for me! What is your problem, you psychotic lady?"

"I don't have a problem, except that you are excessively loud, rude, immature, and selfish creatures who have invaded this wondrous space."

Ms. Shabah's jaw dropped at this rude behavior, and without thought at all, she slapped the woman square across her face. Carol Farrow's eyes filled with tears, and her face seemed permanently stuck in a state of shock and confusion.

29

"Call me a creature again, you mentally ill woman. If you do not stop these 'letters' that you write, I will file for harassment, and you can kiss your kids goodbye as you go to jail. I am sure that they will kiss you back good riddance. I am a woman with respectable children that will not accept abuse from another woman of equally respectable children."

Carol Farrow stared at the lady for a short moment, and then, with a blank expression, slammed the door in her face. Ms. Shabah turned back to go home, storming off the property. She had noticed that Gabriel and Andra had witnessed what happened and smiled in surprise.

When she arrived back home, she was met with her children in the kitchen, when she brushed off her white silk dress of dirt and bacteria. She looked at the children, who stood in front of her in silence, and asked them if they wanted a breakfast meal of omelet and French toast since she had bought the ingredients two days prior. They smiled and agreed, sitting down in the comfortable grey chairs at the round marble table near the kitchen, where they gossiped about their mother. Ms. Shabah couldn't help but smile as she dipped slices of brioche in an egg-sugar mixture, realizing that her actions could finally have ended this troubling woman's career as a secret-telling scribe.

❋　　❋　　❋

Later in the afternoon, Ms. Shabah went on a walk outside hoping to find Ms. Kabila once more. In perfect luck, Ms. Kabila was walking right past her house, wearing a brown fur coat and once again walking her small, loud white dog. She smelled of sweet chocolate, lofting around the street before settling into a thinner odor as she continued to walk. Once Ms. Shabah had caught up with her, she seemed to smile wider, puffing her cheeks into the size of large apples.

"Hello, Ms. Kabila! How do you do?" said Ms. Shabah, asking in a mood such that she was in a rush to talk about something else.

"Great, dear. I just finished the new recipe for apple pie that you had given me last time we talked. Just making my usual walk. How have you been the past couple of days?"

"Relatively well. Only one exception. The lady across the street, Carol Farrow, had written another letter. I'm not sure if you received it or not, but the contents were agonizing."

"I did receive her letter, but never looked at it conscientiously. Explain to me, what are the contents?"

"They detailed my daughter! She had broken her ankle badly, to where she won't be able to walk for a while longer. The lady wrote the letter about her screaming, insisting that it was obnoxious! I thought that she couldn't have been serious, so I walked up to her front door and asked her what she meant by the letter. Oh gosh, Ms. Kabila, you will not believe her answer!"

"Well, tell me! I need to know!"

"Well, she basically ridiculed me! I exposed her to her face, stating exactly what she was in the wrong for, but her expressions and reactions seemed to laugh at me! So, I did what any mother would have done. I slapped that egotistic lady across her face!" said Ms. Shabah, standing proud and tall.

"Ha! Well done, dear!" said Ms. Kabila, laughing at what she had just heard. She seemed genuinely excited about Ms. Shabah's actions and sought a plan while they walked a while longer, talking about nonsense.

"Dearest, I have been thinking about a plan to further what you did and finally end this woman's interests in you and your family. I think she needs a taste of her own medicine, and gift her with exactly what she gifts us," said Ms. Kabila. Ms. Shabah seemed animate her face like a small child on the morning of Christmas. She so eagerly wanted to hear her plan, and Ms. Kabila told her. They both smiled at each other, laughing quietly at the foolishness but genius of what they had formulated.

"Tomorrow, dear, you will see exactly what I talked about in action. It will be tangible! Trust me."

CHAPTER V

On the next morning, the children and Ms. Shabah awoke in their best moods. The birds chirped songs in the distant trees, the sunlight shone perfectly across their house, and the light was absorbed by the inside of the house through the transparent windowpanes, causing a crispy and warm feeling.

Gabriel awoke in a bed of warmth, feeling particularly limber as he strode out of bed. As he opened the door, a fresh scent of lavender and cake migrated deep within his lungs, his mouth watering. As he stepped forward, Cassandra's door opened, and she too inhaled intensely, bringing a large smile to her face. She limped forward to go down the stairs with Gabriel, where they were greeted by their mother in a silky summer dress, enhancing the orange color of her hair as it reflected around the room.

Fresh bouquets of lavender were placed on the dining table, where pancakes also lay, exciting the children. Ms. Shabah thought it would be a perfect day—one without the bleak and maddening Lady Farrow.

The day seemed filled with activities and lessons. After breakfast, Ms. Shabah asked their romance language tutor to immediately come over to review some grammar rules in Spanish and French, as well as a small part in Latin. The children had an authentic response to the tutor today— a rare occasion that occurs almost once every blue moon. Ms. Shabah was quite proud of their reactions. Afterward, the children spoke in French to their mother while they prepared for their trip to the park. They each arrived at the serene location—filled with blossom trees, benches of spruce wood, and a small stream encircling the field of grass that lay ahead on this sunny day—each bringing a book with them to read. Gabriel decided to bring War and Peace, an undertaking that he has attempted for years over. He felt that this year was the prime time to restart his commencement on this read, and he had just finished another book of grandeur right before school finished, which had a lasting effect on him and his writing:

Middlemarch. War and Peace was significantly larger, but conquering Middlemarch was a feat similar in impressiveness.

Cassandra had brought a wonderfully short book, titled The Stranger. She had decided to bring the French copy, L'Étranger, where she could practice her skills of reading the language furthermore. It was a book that she had already read, but she felt as if it were the perfect time to read it again; she had never read it in French.

Ms. Shabah had decided to bring a book that she had begun reading since she had arrived here. It was Wuthering Heights, a book she felt was tragically romantic. However, the main premise of the book seemed to contradict her original beliefs—something that didn't quite make sense on the external.

After a few hours, they arrived back at their home in Quintbridge. Once they pulled into the driveway, they noticed one of the most shocking discoveries they had seen since they first came here.

The letterbox of the Farrow Household had been flooded with letters that organized themselves into a large pile on the ground. It was clear that it had been taken inside since a small trail of letters, presumably from the hands of someone who grabbed a bunch and dropped a few, was left. On this faithful day, Ms. Shabah had asked her lovely son to run up and take a letter from the letterbox, and immediately bring it to her. When he did, the letter read as the exact copy of the letter that Lady Farrow had sent out most recently, except that its regards were by Ms. Kabila.

Ms. Shabah laughed out loud at the plan that had been executed by the vivacious Ms. Kabila. She couldn't help herself, covering her mouth in glee as her children looked on at her confusedly. She told her children, "Originally, the plan was told to me by Ms. Kabila to stop Carol Farrow and her terrible habit. Instead, it seemed to ridicule her! She had told me that she was going to make thousands of copies of the letters—replicas! —and bring them to her letterbox to show her that she is ridiculous. It indeed worked!"

CHAPTER VI

Lady Farrow hadn't bothered the Shabah family or any other resident for an entire week. It had been peace among the mail, where no letters of ill harm were directed at anyone. Not only that, but the sun was shining especially bright, giving rays to the areas of dim light so they could glow lighter. The trees were beginning to grow a less dark green, where they absorbed less of the light, and the world of Quintbridge seemed beautiful once again.

It was as if a deciduous forest had decided to take its course of early spring, where instead of the plethora of leaves lining the trees in the summer, the bare beginnings of growth had appeared. The sun also seemed to keep its radiation levels lower, so the neighborhood could thrive amongst low temperatures

Gabriel Shabah wanted to take advantage of this weather and with the absence of the insufferable Carol Farrow, he went outside to walk around the neighborhood once again. It was immediately after he had taught the Turkish March to Jason on the piano, leaving him with an abundance of time for leisure considering Jason is a fast learner. Alone, without the company of his fantastic sister, he went to the Farrow household to retrieve a special human being.

As he snuck to the left of the house, he noticed in the windowpane furthest above the house was Cassandra, lounging by the invisible wall, collaging in her sketchbook, holding a large book with fine print. She cut out pieces of film and photographs from a magazine and glued them to her papers. She had a face of engrossment in her work, perfectly lining each snip of the magazine and perfectly gluing them down. Gabriel needed her attention, for he wanted to resume his introduction! It was terribly cut off from his sister—her unfortunate injury causing an immediate stop—and he needed to see what else this neighborhood was capable of.

He snuck around the side of her house, reaching for tiny pebbles on the ground and preparing to throw them. He gathered a few and launched them directly for her. The first two didn't make it quite close to the window, but the third made a direct hit—right next to her head.

34

Surprisingly, she had almost no reaction. Gabriel groaned in frustration, although he did notice that she looked particularly beautiful concentrating like that.

He tried again, and after making two more consecutive hits, she finally looked out the window. Her face rejuvenated at the sight of him standing below her house, ushering her to sneak out to come to walk with him. She nodded in agreement, shrugged her shoulders, and smiled in a state of extreme excitement. Gabriel's cheeks pulled on his face, forcing a genuine smile. He did not realize he had smiled, however, and it caused him a slight confusion.

In what almost seemed like an instant, she crawled through the small opening underneath her house, stood up, and brushed the dust off her light pink dress. She laughed while she called his name in surprise and pranced over before hugging him. Gabriel thought it was a little extraneous but found comfort in her company.

"Cassandra, I have been thinking…, and we never finished our introduction! You must show me the rest of the neighborhood!"

"Well, of course! I would be delighted to escort you, Gabriel. But I must ask, are we walking alone or shall we bring your sister along? I know she is completely absorbed with her terrible injury, but I feel like she must be allowed to come with us."

"Ah, of course. However, I feel it best that she doesn't walk. Plus, she would only slow us down!"

"Yes, yes, I assume you are right. Let's begin then!" Cassandra said as she began leading Gabriel down the same pathway where the Ledgers were located. "Technically, after the Ledger's Household, there is only one family that is actually worthy of being introduced to you, dearest. Specifically, the girl of our age in the family. Her name is Delilah. I absolutely adore her. We go to the same school."

"Ah, well that should be exciting! I love meeting new people, and you seem to have the best taste in people, honestly!"

"Well, thank you, kind sir," said she, smiling and blushing quietly by their side,

They enjoyed nature together. Each of the calls of the birds echoing in this small paradise seemed to allow them to feel more connected. Gabriel made a mental note that it felt like he was walking through heaven's gate, where the nature and energy of the situation seemed appropriately incredible. Cassandra felt as if the world was turning in her favor; she hadn't had the best luck with neighbors, exclusively with romantic attractions. Gabriel seemed perfect for her.

When they continued down the same road that the faithful event of Andra's ankle had occurred, they noticed that the same group of boys was riding their boards around. The only exception was that Jason was not a part of it. Once one of them noticed that the pair was walking in their direction, the group immediately ran over, asking if their dear Andra was okay.

"Yes, boys, she is perfectly fine. Can barely walk, but she should heal," said Gabriel.

"Thank God! I have been hoping that there was hope in her situation. Gabriel, Cassandra, I am not sure you understand. We were terrified. When she was screaming, we felt as if we had almost caused an accidental murder!" said one of the Ledgers

"Oh, no worries. Broken bones happen all the time. It just happens to be that Andra is particularly fragile."

"Good to know! Now, you both must tell me, what are you doing on this side of the neighborhood? Has Quintbridge influenced you to try skateboarding again?" said the eldest Ledger boy.

"Ha-ha-ha, no. I wanted another introduction to the rest of the neighborhood. It seems Cassandra never gave it to me in full because of what happened with my sister."

"Apologies! But today we are meeting my best friend—you all know her! She and you will definitely connect!" said Cassandra, punching Gabriel in the shoulder in a joking manner.

"Ah, well it seems exciting! You will love her Gabriel; truly the nicest girl I have ever met," said one of the Ledgers.

"And attractive too!" said another.

"Well, I shall see for myself. Bye for now! I hope to ride the skateboards again, just without fault!" said Gabriel.

Afterward, the boys seemed to skate in a livelier manner, feeling quite relieved as they had received news of Andra's inclining health condition. Gabriel and Cassandra trotted away as they talked about nonsense on the way to the girl's house. Gabriel felt ever-so-curious about who exactly she was because she seemed to make an absolute impact on everyone she had encountered.

When they arrived at the said location, her house seemed rather worn-out in comparison to the rest of the houses nearby. It had scars and scratches on the sides of the house unlike any that Gabriel had seen. Cassandra explained how it was because she had such a large family, that there was always some small calamity occurring, and that the house had already been under construction four times in the past year for some destruction to its interior or exterior.

Once they knocked on the door, she opened it, yelling some Spanish before returning to the door with an awkward smile.

"Well, hello! Who are you?" asked the young girl

"Delilah, this is Gabriel. He is the new arrival in the neighborhood, and he asked me to give him an introduction to the best members of society that Quintbridge has to offer. Delilah, this is Gabriel Shabah, and Gabriel, this is Delilah Candella," said Cassandra.

They both shook hands, Delilah with a kind smile on her face, and Gabriel with a nervous look.

"So very pleased to meet you!" said she.

"Absolutely the same. You are perfection reincarnated."

"Well thank you, kind sir. I am happy to know you now. Cassandra and—you—, I am so sorry that I cannot speak long! I have some business to attend to with my younger siblings. I must talk with you again! *En seria*," said Delilah Candella before she quietly shut the door with a smile. Afterward, there was some loud yelling in Spanish, and they walked away through the soft yard.

"You know, I have become quite knowledgeable about the Spanish language. It is quite fascinating. I take many lessons at my house with my mother and sister. We are learning Spanish, Arabic, and French at the moment, although, I am plunging into a small bit of German and Italian in secret."

"That is indeed fascinating, Gabriel! You do astound me every time I hear a fact about you."

"Well, speaking of being astounded, that girl has entirely astounded me. I have never felt what I have felt for her when seeing someone for the first time."

Cassandra seemed to become slightly sullen, playing with the skin in her palms and looking lower to the ground. "Oh, that is interesting. You truly haven't felt like that for anyone else?"

"No, I have not."

"Oh…"

"Yes—but I must tell you, I need to know about everything to do with that girl. Delilah Candella. Her name reminds me of the book Lolita, where in the first few lines, he sounds the first name in syllables. De-li-lah. So beautiful."

"She is quite the beautiful person, yes. She is also accomplished too. She is the valedictorian at our high school, incredibly intelligent, the lead in multiple plays and musicals, has a singing voice so spectacular that it is capable of making you cry, and she has a job at the local farmer's market. The girl is an inspiration," said Cassandra, trembling her voice as she explained the facts of Delilah Candella, the new love-of-his-life.

It saddened her entirely when she heard his words about the beautiful girl. Cassandra felt as if she had been getting played against this entire afternoon, considering his enticing smile earlier, his words of compliments, and every other action or movement he had done. She felt like a harp, leaning hard into someone that only wanted to play around with her strings. Cassandra did not want to be with Gabriel any longer and felt it best to go on her way home.

"Gabriel, I am not feeling quite well. I think the sun is causing a slight headache for me, and I want to go home. Let's go back?"

"Yes, absolutely. The last thing I would want is for you to faint under the pressures of the sun. I shall walk you back!"

As they began their way back toward the Farrow household, Cassandra stopped in her tracks suddenly. In the distance, a man and his hound were jogging in their direction; a face on the man so stern that he seemed angry and cold. He switched from the left side of the road to the right side of the road, directly towards the pair.

"Oh, God! Do you see that man? We must hide! —Gabriel, hide with me now! Get behind this bush, out of sight, and away from that man!"

Gabriel and Cassandra ran further from the road and into bushes, where the woods began and the yard of a household unknown to them ended. In utter confusion, Gabriel asked Cassandra what exactly was going on, since it seemed as if nothing is wrong with that man.

"Oh, Gabriel, you do not understand! That man, named Popov, is pure evil. There are plenty of rumors circling the neighborhood saying that he has killed people before he moved here, that he sold drugs to get all the money that he had attained, and that dog he is trained to kill! There are so many issues with that man, and so it is custom that when a child of any age, especially female, considering that his past victims had all been female, they must hide. Look at him run!" exclaimed Cassandra.

Gabriel squatted in the woods, huddled with Cassandra, as they watched the Russian man running throughout the neighborhood. He ran with intensity, wearing a beanie and gloves in warm weather. He seemed eerie but also strong. Popov made an immediate impression on Gabriel that he was a dangerous man; Cassandra panted heavily in fear directly next to him. When he noticed, he grabbed her close so that she could feel comforted and not scared of an anomaly of a man. Cassandra smiled at the warmth of his body surrounding her own and thought of what this truly meant. She believed he might have been exaggerating about the delightful Delilah Candella.

Almost two minutes after Popov and his hound had run past, Cassandra and Gabriel made their journey back home at a much faster pace. She had installed some fear in the boy, in hopes that Popov would return so he could hold her again. Unfortunately for her, he never arrived again. Once Gabriel and Cassandra came back home, they bid each other adieu and went back inside their respective homes for the night.

Cassandra Farrow thought of Gabriel and what he was actively thinking of her. Gabriel simply thought of Delilah Candella, the most majestic and irresistibly elegant young girl he had ever laid his eyes upon.

CHAPTER VII

The door to the Shabah household opened and closed rather quickly, with Gabriel bursting through the doorway. He fluttered his way upstairs towards the room on top of the garage: Cassandra Shabah's beautifully decorated bedroom. She had pink flowering details stemming from each corner and crevice in her room; a print of a portrait of a young lady painted within the early seventeenth or eighteenth century hung above her pillowy and soft bed; a collage of Cassandra's favorite musical artists and fashion icons was made close to the mirror where her makeup had been perfectly prepared for the next day: it was a room of comfort and solitude perfectly mixed within a space of rest and relaxation.

Cassandra sat on a small sofa, listening to her record player, her legs crossed in a state of comfort, and a book with a red cover (presumably Jane Eyre, a book which Cassandra had just read recently but loved) between her fingers as she read intensely.

She noticed that once Gabriel stepped into the room, panting at both distress of the event with the man outside and the exercise that he had just completed with the stairs, there was something urgent. "What are you doing in my room, Gabriel? Why are you huffing in here so loudly?"

"Oh god, Cassandra! I have just experienced the most awful event I have had yet in this neighborhood—"

"Oh please, stop exaggerating! Enough of this! What could it have been?"

"Cassandra, there was a man! He had a dog with him, unleashed, running right behind him!" He talked in speedy language, speaking at an incomprehensible pace.

"Gabriel, you need to slow down! Did this man injure you?" asked the girl, now properly sat up and not listening to anything as she paid her full willing attention to the words he had to say.

"No, no, he did not injure me. However, there was something direr that I must warn you about. Cassandra told me that the man was evil—a murderer! He had killed many children in the past and would be

40

completely able to do it again—especially with us! Cassandra, make sure to stay away from him—he chased Cassandra and me in the neighborhood and ran directly towards us—I thought he was going to kill us like Cassandra said he had done in the past!"

"Oh, Gabriel, you need to calm it! This is not a threat; the man seems to simply be running. I have already seen him when I went to Jason's house for fencing—he is only running!" said she.

"I'm not so certain. Cassandra told me—"

"Gabriel, stop! Cassandra may have lived here, but she does not know all."

"Humph, ok. I need to calm down," he said, taking deep breaths to reach serenity. "In other sorts of news, when I was out completing my introduction with Cassandra Farrow, I met the loveliest girl! Her name is Delilah Candella, which is incredibly pretty for just a name, and my goodness, she is immaculate! She is by far the prettiest and most intelligent girl I've ever met, surpassing even the greatest celebrities and figures of my imagination that I have ever known. I wanted to tell you this because—because—," Gabriel paused for a short while before resuming, "—because I feel as if I might be in love with her."

"Gabriel, what? You have only just met her—"

"Yes, I am aware, but I don't know, I just feel as if I had immediately seen the one who I have wanted all my life. There is a morality in her, a morality that is so unlike the rest of the world, simple yet complex, similar yet different. We only exchanged a short number of words, but her sentences created what seemed to be a resounding passion for living. Her kindness was unlike any other person I have met during the first instance of meeting them, and I just feel compelled to her! I'm not sure why I am telling you things; perhaps it is because I want you to know that there is some worth to this place. The deadly and ugly are not so bad once you find the small drop of honey between them. Or so I think," equivocated Gabriel, who seemed utterly infatuated with the girl.

Cassandra stood shocked. She seemed to think that something had happened to Gabriel and that his reason for acting like such is because he has been delusional since arriving here. He had such a heavy pessimism that anything remotely opposite is deemed as pure worth. Cassandra thought he was ridiculous but hoped that one day he would learn that his thoughts made no sense. Why, all of a sudden, did Gabriel believe that he was in love with a girl he had just met? And why had he believed that this man running throughout the neighborhood every day at noon was somehow a detriment to life for young children?

Although, one thing did seem to stick out like a sore thumb to Cassandra about Gabriel. He seemed genuinely happier here. He seemed to have found a means to understand his position in the world and seemed truly content with it.

Cassandra also noticed that Cassandra Farrow was also seemingly acting differently. She had a deep, unforgiving love for Gabriel—on a level such that women are only able to detect. Gabriel was utterly oblivious to such, but Cassandra saw it. She saw exactly how she buzzed around him like a bee encountering the most supreme nectar of the flower field; how she would talk as if it were her last moments with him, and that she wanted to remain brutally honest with her words; how there was such an insignificant but frequent touch that she would perform on Gabriel, each second, but without his regard.

However, her thoughts were interrupted by the call of her mother, asking loudly from below the stairs if Gabriel had come home yet. Gabriel answered for himself, which prompted the woman to order him downstairs along with Cassandra immediately. They both arrived in the kitchen where, leaning against the countertop, was their mother, visibly upset.

"I do not want to continue talking about this subject, but it is of far importance to me, and you must listen closely and attentively. You both, and under no circumstances, will ever see the young Cassandra Farrow again," said she.

"But mother, I—"

"No circumstances! Gabriel, I understand the friendship that you have furthered with her today, and I understand that I was very fond of the girl for an extended period of time, but there will be no further negotiation surrounding this. She is to be out of my sights and out of yours!"

"Oh mother, why?" asked Cassandra.

"There is one magnitude of a reason which should explain everything. Today, I received news from Ms. Kabila that there was a talk going around—a talk of us, again. Carol Farrow, that wretched woman, was stating to the neighbors nearby that she has made a family compact to be formally against us—like we are in some psychotic war!" said Ms. Shabah, as she began to sob. "She has said that she wants us out of the neighborhood entirely, and she, along with her entire family, is calling for support from the neighborhood. Not only that, but several people have agreed to take her side on this. I am eliciting a visceral reaction of anger, something that I cannot control. Oh, children, you must understand! I want to commit murder sometimes when I hear the stories of this woman!"

"Mother," said Gabriel, "we are completely on your side, and we stand in solidarity with you! Do not fret in the slightest. Regarding her disgusting comments about our family being ousted by the neighborhood—it will never happen. Mother don't sob! We are going to be perfectly well in here!"

Ms. Shabah sobbed loudly, placing her palms on her eyes as her fingers curled through her hair. She has a black smudge running down her soft, aged cheek. Her crying had caused the young Cassandra to also cry with her, and the women huddled together, feeling, and experiencing each other's emotions. Their companionship took a large effect on Gabriel, as he vowed to always follow her orders to not see her again.

After the crying had passed and the family had settled, Ms. Shabah had excused herself to find Ms. Kabila on the road for a walk-and-talk. However, to the surprise of both Ms. Shabah and her children, she arrived back after a couple of minutes, not being able to find Ms. Kabila.

"How strange! She is always on the same schedule for her walk, and the last time we spoke, she mentioned nothing about how this day in particular would conflict with it! I wonder if she is to come later," exclaimed Ms. Shabah.

She retrieved some water and a lawn chair, and sat on her driveway, staying hydrated and cool while she waited. After more than half an hour, longer than Ms. Shabah would have expected Ms. Kabila to be tardy, she walked back inside. Ms. Kabila never showed up at her house that afternoon or walked in the neighborhood at all. Ms. Shabah found it a little peculiar.

CHAPTER VIII

In the evening of the next day, Ms. Shabah sent her daughter to fencing lessons with the handsome Jason next door, who was already entering the "fifty best fencers in the country" list. Jason's starry eyes and creased smile encouraged Cassandra Shabah to focus deeply on her fencing skills. His angelic nature and his strong, masculine energy seemed to infatuate her as she thought of him before entering his house. When she arrived, she made sure to give three strong knocks and perfect her hair quickly before the door opened, hoping she could see his face immediately instead of his mother's, who she would need to slip past to get to her boy.

Bonnie stood there; her lipstick half smeared on her face and a small glass of wine in her hand. She invited her into the house and asked her if she wanted anything to drink, hinting toward the wine. Of course, Cassandra did not agree to this, thinking it was quite inappropriate. Jason appeared, seeming particularly happy about seeing her today. She followed the boy downstairs to the basement, where a neat setup of fencing materials was laid out.

He sat in the corner of the room, evaluating the position of the materials and pieces of equipment that he had laid out. Cassandra twirled her hair and pranced towards him, giggling subtly when she noticed his shock at her sudden movement. She greeted him, saying how this was going to be "so much fun" and that she "couldn't wait" in her most flirtatious tone of voice. However, she felt like a fool when she reached out for a hug and was received with his hand, ready to shake hers, establishing the situation as professional.

Cassandra seemed to like him, and when she sat in her room pondering about what they could be, her love for him expanded. She would dream about him, think about him as she ate cereal, and feel his presence looming over her when she recognized her ankle's state. The boy seemed to haunt her, and when they finally had some time alone to be with each other, he wanted to take everything so seriously. She wished it was a joking, sarcastic manner like when they were on the skateboard. Now, she noticed the pain in her ankle growing, intensifying

44

as if something was slowly stabbing into a bruise. It was probably the result of her prancing.

When she opened her palm and joined his regrettably, he pulled her in close, and hugged her, saying that he missed her and couldn't wait to begin lessons.

"I'm only joking. Why would I handshake you? We are alone, after all! I hope your ankle isn't in too much pain. If it is such trouble, we can just watch a movie instead," said he.

"No, I am fine. Let's begin the lesson, I suppose. I have never done anything in fencing before, and I find the sport quite fascinating. It is like watching someone duel with another; it's reminiscent of the early ages. I'm glad to have you as my teacher!" she said flirtatiously, again.

Once she had readied herself in her fencing suit and stood in the center of the basement with her épée in hand, she looked at Jason, puzzled.

"Well, strike the dummy!" said Jason.

She turned to face the rubber mannequin. It was simply a torse, no arms, legs, or even head. She attempted to slice it with her flimsy sword, trying her best to cut it open. A sigh was released from Jason as he stepped toward her.

"What did I do wrong?" asked Cassandra.

"Have you ever seen the sport before? You don't strike at it, attempting to slice and dice the dummy. The épée isn't built for that. You need to stab it. Let me show you," he said.

He stood behind her, mere inches from her suit that made her sweat so profusely. He then moved his right arm down her right arm, squatted to match her height, and began moving it about. The weapon flailed in the air for a few moments as he began to get used to her feeling.

He then seemed to caress her, moving ever so slightly, having his hands touch her softly. He guided her in the direction of the dummy and stabbed it directly into the center rapidly. It surprised Cassandra how fast she had moved without anticipating it. He whispered in her ear a few remarks about how well she is doing and asked her to do it on her own, removing himself from the area in which they stood.

Cassandra longed for the weight and warmth of his body to be back on her, but she mimicked the movements he taught her. On the first attempt, she had perfectly stabbed the épée into the dummy.

"Why, that was perfect, Cassandra! You did incredibly!"

"Thank you, kind sir. Although, I do have one question. If this is an épée, why do you have a dummy that is simply a torso? The foil is the type of weapon that must be used for a torso. Even a saber, which only regards the upper body, is better suited for this type of equipment. Why are you making me practice with an épée?" she asked inquisitively.

"Well, I did not think about that. I have always used this for practicing with an épée, and it has seemed to work splendidly."

"Well, maybe, perhaps…, you could suit up and have proper practice with me?" Cassandra was nervous about his response. She had never been so forward and blunt in her life, especially with a boy.

"Sure. Give me a moment then," he said, and raced to his room, leaving Cassandra alone.

She lifted her mask and thought to herself how wonderful this opportunity is going to be with him. She was extremely excited to see him in all his glory, and her thoughts of this made her smile. It startled her when her face began moving slightly, but she acquiesced and allowed it to continue like that.

After a minute or so, the boy walked back downstairs, dressed in a clean fencing suit. He had his mask pulled down and asked her to do the same. She did.

"Ok, so this is how this is going to go. I am going to stand on this side of the basement, while you stand on the other side of the basement. Then, when I say go, we will both begin lunging and attacking and defending etcetera. When I try to stab you, make sure you deflect my weapon. You can hit me anywhere on the body at all. Most importantly, be honest if I strike you or if you strike me. First to ten?"

"Yes, sounds good. I'm ready to start whenever."

"Ok. Three, two, one, go!"

Immediately, they got into position, and Cassandra could not stop giggling. Jason had taken this much more seriously than she had expected. He began lunging and flailing his épée in the air around her. Soon enough, she felt a small, pointy feeling in her shin, and she burst out laughing.

"Be serious, Andra!" said he, laughing with her. However, she could not contain herself, and she slowly bent down lower until she seemed like she was about to assume the fetal position. Jason laughed with her and picked her up.

He lifted her mask and looked deeply into her eyes which watered from the deep bellows of laughter. Something compelled him to lift his mask too, and slowly move toward her face. Her laughs slowed

46

to what sounded like hiccups, and then they slowed to nothing. She looked just as innocently back at him. She felt the urge to lean in, and so she did. They were mere inches from each other's faces when Bonnie suddenly knocked on the door.

"Cassandra Shabah! Your mother! I had just seen her crying—she shouted at the Farrow lady—she is storming off to her house now—get going! You need to go! You must go see your mother! She looks in dire condition," hurried Bonnie in a slur of words. Cassandra peered over to look at her concerned face smothered in lipstick. The corners of her mouth, slightly opened and drooping downwards, also stained in a thin layer of wine, confirmed that something dire indeed had happened.

Immediately, Cassandra took off her outfit and ran back upstairs. She issued a very quick goodbye to Jason, who seemed discombobulated by the situation which had just occurred.

Cassandra ran out of the front door and walked at a hasty speed back towards her house. In the corner of her eye, as if something was intruding on her vision, she saw a girl running down her driveway with two young boys.

Cassandra Farrow and the Lillis twins were running quickly down the driveway, looking over their shoulders in hopes of not being seen by someone in the house. Before they had begun their sprint, Cassandra and Cassandra made eye contact.

Cassandra Farrow's face seemed to bleed; a bruise swelled on her eye and a gash appeared on the side of her cheek. She seemed to be completely beaten up. Her mouth was left agape, and her teary eyes seemed stuck frozen when she saw the Shabah girl. Cassandra Farrow appeared to have just lost everything and was beaten unapologetically afterward. It worried the Shabah girl. Cassandra Farrow had just lost her family and had to resort to staying with the only people she did not like. She had a sullen face, one of complete despair but also mixed with shock and fear, and she stared directly at Cassandra Shabah.

In comparison, Cassandra Shabah's face was plagued with worry but also blessed with happiness. She had just achieved what she had always wanted. The girl had never been entangled with a boy whom she had deeply appreciated, and now she had exactly that. She also seemed to have a care to give, a risk that some people—Cassandra Farrow, in particular—did not have the privilege of having. Care is only something that someone can give if they have space to lose. Her worry consisted of her mother and the girl that looked at her now.

The Lillis twins tugged on the long denim skirt that Cassandra Farrow was wearing, and she broke eye contact. She ran off into the distance, seemingly nowhere but with the certainty of a destination in mind. Cassandra Shabah seemed confused and scared for the girl, but she had forgotten it relatively quickly because she had to attend to her mother so urgently.

✳   ✳   ✳

"Mother? Are you doing well? What is wrong? Why are you crying?" asked Cassandra, who seemed to heighten the pitch in her voice once noticing the true trouble of her mother.

"Oh, my sweet, sweet child. I am in despair! The biggest evil in this neighborhood is carrying a deep hatred for us! That dreaded Farrow mother!"

"Oh, mother! What happened?"

"I shall tell you exactly, as my memory is still fresh and able to recall this exact conversation," said Ms. Shabah. She prepared to tell the girl exactly what had transpired at the Farrow household while the girl had gone to her fencing lesson.

"I looked out of my window and noticed the Farrow woman standing by her garden; she picked small weeds and tended to her tulips that had been previously destroyed by myself. I am aware that that was wrong, but in the heat of the moment, I did not care about destroying them. I had a strange idea to expose and understand exactly what Lady Farrow had intended by her compact. Immediately, I prepared a large mug of coffee, filling it to the halfway mark to create an illusion that I had been drinking it throughout the day, so I didn't seem like a maniac. I then set on my course toward the Farrow household. As I entered the driveway, I began to call out,

'Good afternoon, Lady Farrow. I wanted to ask you some questions if you aren't too busy?' She then replied:

'I guess you can. I am tending to my garden, though. I am a small part busy—'

I cut her off mid-sentence. 'Well, it is going to be quick, so there shouldn't be anything to worry about,' is what I said. I know that it was quite rude, but I was in an urgent state. She then said,

'Okay. What exactly do you want to know?' to which I replied, 'Oh, well, I have been hearing gossip—which I unquestionably hate to hear—and I wanted to understand what you meant. I have heard that

48

you have created a compact with your family to hate us until we are gone and that you are actively looking for signatures to make us leave our property. I want to know if this is true?'"

Ms. Shabah took a small break to let out some cries that had been pushing their way through her throat. Cassandra snuggled up next to her mother, warming her with her deep worry. She seemed extraordinarily distressed about this story considering the level her mother cried. Ms. Shabah felt a small lump occur in her trachea, but she continued,

"'Well, if it wasn't true, that is definitely some rumor,' said Lady Farrow, smiling as she picked a couple of tulips in her hand and smelled them deeply. She had seemed to have taken a dislike to the flowers and decided to cut them all from the garden. I was getting angry, and that comment sparked something in me, so I said,

'Ah, so you truly have a vendetta against us, don't you? Is it because we have taken the more lovely house that you wished you had? Or is it because we have been so utterly kind to the rest of the neighbors here that they seem to like us better?' What had captivated me! I then took a few intimidating steps closer to Lady Farrow and continued: 'We have been nothing but kind, and I can't help but not comprehend why you hate us so much! I feel that there is something terribly wrong with you, and so many other people have told me the same. They told me all the disgusting comments you make about us, the stories you say, and the jealousy that flows through your sickening veins.' She replied,

'Well, if you don't mind, get out of my property! I don't want to hear your weird sentences and extraneous thoughts. I already have enough on my plate just hearing you breathe across from my very exquisite home!' How dare she! How insulting is that my dear Cassandra! I stood my ground and replied:

'Well, maybe I won't leave. There is too much to talk about with you, especially about that disgusting mouth of yours.' I noticed that Lady Farrow's eldest daughter and son were staring at me from the windowpane, and, if I am to be honest, I got nervous. I didn't want to seem like that, however, so I retaliated and continued, 'I see your minions have arrived to stare at me.' She then said,

'Well, maybe it's best you leave! I don't want to argue with you!' I should have listened instead of being a drama, but I did not. I called her out exactly, and said,

'Stop spreading hate comments about me and my family!' She then said,

'You stop causing me to say those things!' So, I yelled back,

49

'No, you erratic woman! You are totally in the wrong, so admit it!' I was getting increasingly angry at the woman, but then she said the biggest insult I have ever heard,

'I shall not apologize for anything. You are the evil here that needs to be expelled! Look at yourself, your ugly figure, and your dumb children. It's a shame my daughter has been infected by your gross genetics. I have a theory that your bacteria is as poisonous as the Elephant's Foot in Chernobyl! Everyone else I talked to believes it too! You stole everything. Your presence ruins everything here! Get out of this neighborhood!' I felt tears in my eyes, never hearing as much hate directed at me as ever before, and so I cried out in desperation,

'I literally have done nothing! You have lost your mind, truly— lost it! I am disgusted to have you as my neighbor!' I left the premises after that comment, and ran back home hastily, spilling my coffee at each stride. That is when I started sobbing and wept at the thought of someone containing pure hatred for me for no particular reason at all. What drove the woman to hate our family felt bizarre and unusual and made me quite sad, and so here I am! Sobbing my eyes out! Oh, Cassandra, I have never felt this way. How can someone hate someone else without logic or reason? It seemed like she had been possessed by the devil himself. I moved here to restart and to give you and Gabriel an opportunity. It's a damned shame that it has been taken by an evil witch like her!"

Cassandra was positively shocked. She could do nothing except comfort her mother in a time of desperation and ponder exactly the conversation. The way the Farrow woman released slurs and insults so easily made her shiver.

Nothing had prepared Cassandra for what she had just heard, but upon hearing it, she noticed something. Her mother had stated that the Farrow lady had mentioned that her daughter—Cassandra Farrow—had been infected by the Shabah. Just earlier, Andra recalled that Gabriel had spent some time with the girl. The bruises seemed to make more sense: it was her mother! She had indefinitely hit the Farrow girl and left a multitude of bruises and gashes on her. The Lillis twins must have been the final resort for her, considering Gabriel could not be allowed to speak to her any longer.

Gabriel walked downstairs and seeing her concerned facial expression of Cassandra and hearing the sounds of his mother's cries, he immediately embraced them. Only later would he hear the news of what had made his mother so upset.

It was a warm comfort; to sit in a room holding and grasping each other in a sea of emotion is what made this feeling so warm. Although dread and grief had begun settling deep within the Shabah family, their hugging had proved that they would stick together. A fire, holding the sticks of its growth together by its hot force, had arisen within the Shabah. It was a strong fire, wildly uncontrollable and unmalleable. However, a few short spouts of water frequented their fire, testing its strength. The Shabah had been shoved and pushed all their life, but nothing exactly seemed to defy them as much as the Farrow family had.

CHAPTER IX

After a few hours of tender embrace by the Shabah family, and after Ms. Shabah had calmed down entirely, Andra stood up. She had attempted to find her jacket which she was wearing when she went to her fencing lesson. However, she was unable to find it and turned to her mother.

"Mother, I know that this isn't really something that you want to hear, but could I please go back to Jason's house and retrieve my jacket? I had left it there during my fencing lesson, and I am freezing," said she. Andra had no particular interest in seeing Jason for the second time in one day, but she truly wanted to get her jacket back. She was nervous that Ms. Shabah was going to decline her request because it would be inappropriate. Andra did want her jacket back though, and it was an expensive silk zip-up: something that she had wanted since she was young and only received a year or so ago.

"Is that really necessary?"

"Yes, mother, I do need it. It's my silk one!"

"Well, I suppose so. Don't stay out late though. I do not want you interacting with those Farrow people tonight."

"Yes, mother, of course. I would never interact with them anyways; I was not ever too fond of Cassandra."

She made her way back out of the house, watching as the two fire-headed twins ran back downstairs with papers in each of their hands. They also had a small contraption, similar to the size of a calculator.

"What are you two rascals doing with those papers? Why are you holding something that looks like a calculator? What is that?" questioned Andra to the Lillis twins.

"Well—they are nun' o' your business, ain't they? But we'll tell ya'. It is *calicus* paper, or maths, whatever. Cassandra needed 'em. This is a calculator, we thinks. Also, our grammar is awful, apologies," answered the twins.

Andra had noticed that they were unable to spell calculus. She wondered how Cassandra, a girl who seemed not the slightest bit

52

intelligent could be taking a difficult math course in her free time, the summer. Andra thought that she could be genuinely smart, and she recalled a time when Cassandra shared an intelligent observation with the Shabahs. She asked the boys how they got inside, and they only giggled before running back out of their house. One of the boys stopped for a moment and turned to look back at the girl.

"It is late, and we wants ya' to know that Cassandra is hidin' with us. Don't bother lookin' for 'er. Bye!" said the boy, before running back to catch up with his brother.

Andra rolled her eyes at the boys; they were not helping her. She felt that Cassandra was in danger, considering that she was in hiding with the boys. She decided to forget about it, remembering that if all the Farrows had decided to make a compact against them, Cassandra would be involved.

She strolled back down the street, only walking a small distance down the pavement. The ground was smooth, the light low and dark, and the birds chirping throughout the canopies of branches above her. Andra felt at peace in nature, instead of in her own home where chaos bred thoroughly. Nature was a relaxing escape for her, and her love of butterflies, moths, large and colorful birds, the deer that meandered around the woody areas of their neighborhood, and every other animal that set its foot upon the ground here flourished within her.

Sometimes, Andra hoped she could turn into an animal. She wanted to morph into a graceful fawn, only worrying about where to find food and water and learning how to escape from potential danger. Or maybe a seahorse, only being dragged by the power of the feminine ocean, drifting in and out of kelps and grasses, and always looking majestic in the water. She thought about how the worries of the world and how human affairs would simply disappear. They would be an afterthought. The world had a lot more exploring for her to do, and she couldn't do that if she was dragged down by the force of the human tongue. Thus, she filled her room with pink and photos of cute animals, in hopes that one day she could be out of touch with reality in the same form that her room was filled with the embodiment of the absurd for a mature girl. She remembered though, that the true reason she had stayed here is that there was a boy whom she was beginning to love. Each time someone said a sentence, she remembered how he had said one of those words once. The smell of white gardenias that flowed throughout some parts of the neighborhood ignited a memory of his scent. She felt vulnerable around him like she couldn't control her words or actions.

When she arrived at the beginning of the driveway, she heard some calls coming from deep down the road, interrupting her fall into deep thought. It was of her name; a distant 'Andra!' was heard a few times. She turned and squinted, attempting to make out exactly what was in the distance. A few figures of boys had come into her vision, and they were running up to her fast. At first, it reminded her of the warning Gabriel had given her regarding the Russian man that ran around the neighborhood but remembered the familiarity of those voices, so exaggerated in calm and mixed in with a swab of excitement. It was the Ledger boys, who were so eager for her attention. She slowly and intriguingly walked up to them, asking what is wrong.

"Oh, Andra, thank God you are here! We were originally looking for Jason, but you will do just fine. Look what we have found— you must come to look!" exclaimed one of the boys.

"Yes, Andra, come!" said another

Andra hobbled over with them, still walking relatively slowly with the cast on her foot. It didn't hurt constantly as it had before, but it was still painful when she made a sudden movement or if something touched it. When they all arrived at the location, they saw a small dog, like a Chihuahua, eerily skinny and shaking. Layers of dry mud had covered its fur, matting it so it was rock hard and impossible to stroke out. It stood there, plainly terrified by the huddle above it, and looking as if it was just a lost alley dog that had been found by a group of rescuers, attempting to bring it back to its lively personality and clean it so it is attractive and not daunting.

"We think it's Ms. Kabila's," said one of the other boys.

"Why?" asked Andra, biting her fingernails nervously as she examined the state of the dog and its deep petrification of the people surrounding it.

"Well, no one else in the neighborhood that I know of has a teacup poodle like hers. It also is the same cream color as hers, although you can only see the color when you break off some mud."

"Why is it here? Did you bring it here?" asked Andra, concerningly caring for the dog, and hugging it lovingly. She tried to calm it down, but it seemed utterly terrified, and it couldn't stop shaking.

"No, we did not. We have no idea why it is here, but that's why you are here. We know you know Ms. Kabila better than we do, and we wanted you to come with us to ask her what she was thinking."

"Were you not about to ask Jason to come with you?"

"No, we were. He used to dog-sit for her. You seem like a braver option, though. Aren't your mother and her friends?"

"Yes," replied Andra, "but I am not sure how I am supposed to help. Well, I can't even walk a mile with my state right now! I am sure I can help you if you so wish." She paused for a moment and then contradicted her last statement. "Actually, I am not sure if I can. I need to get back home with my mother, and Jason has the silk jacket I'm desperate for. It is quite cold tonight, you know!"

"Yes, we know, but we need you! Look at this poor dog! Ms. Kabila is abusing it, guaranteed! Do you not care?" the boys questioned.

"Oh—I care! Do not accuse me of not. —I guess I can come over there with you guys. However, you are doing all the talking, not me! I don't want to *expose* her or whatever the purpose of this is!" said Andra.

Altogether, they walked down the pavement towards Ms. Kabila's house, dragging the dog along with them with noises of encouragement, like sucking in their pressed lips or making tongue clicks. Andra began to make groans of pain while she was walking, attempting to gather the attention of some of the boys so they could help her walk. She successfully did, and two of the boys attached to her on both sides, holding her by her shoulders and placing her arms around their necks, like a brace for support.

Once they arrived at the house, they noticed that the grass had been particularly long. It had rained for a few days earlier in the week, so the boys and the girl thought it wasn't too unusual that the grass had grown to considerable length. The lights next to the corners of the front door flickered constantly, and a multitude of bugs had been flying around it. The time was relatively late, and Andra thought of how inappropriate this would seem to disturb the old woman; she looked at the dog and reminded herself of what she was here for. If the woman had not been abusive, she might have missed her dog! Andra felt completely entitled to return it.

Ms. Kabila's house was a wonder to see. It was stories high, guarded in marble that shined and glimmered in the daylight or the moonlight, looking excessively clean—almost varnished—than any other house she had seen. It was a masterpiece of architectural design, ranging from jutting stones and corners to smooth, bubble edges. A large amount of purple was seen inside, looking to be a possible couch or a statue of some sort that was painted that way, and the windows were perfectly clean, glossy, and unscratched.

55

Her house was just as perfect as it had always been. Andra was curious as to how she got her money, and if she had spent the large majority customizing the house or if it had been bought exactly like it was at the current moment.

They stepped up to the front of the door.

"Andra, you knock."

"What? No! I said I am not getting involved in this. I am doing this to provide moral support, and I am standing right here," said she, taking a few steps back so her heels were touching the dew in the long grass, prominently wetting her cast.

"Well, I think that we should have a vote as to who knocks. We can't just stand here forever—someone will see us. All who vote Andra knock say 'Aye!'"

"Aye!"

"Aye-aye!"

"Aye!"

"This is not fair," said Andra. "I am not doing that. If you are going to play these games, I will simply leave. I am not going to be told what to do by men, especially *boys*, who had no understanding of class and maturity. I am a Shabah woman, not a pushover."

"Fine. You do it," said the oldest Ledger, lightly pushing the smallest boy that was with them, presumably the youngest brother.

"Yeah, you do it. Aye!"

"Aye!"

"Aye," said Andra hesitantly.

The little boy bravely stepped up to the front door of the house and stood for a moment, shrouded in the silence of nature. It seemed that the Earth had stopped rotating for a moment, the wind halting nervously, the birds pausing their mating calls, and the rest of the people outside Ms. Kabila's front door were gone. The only noise was the slight hum of the lights on the door; electricity could not be halted naturally like the bare globe. The little boy raised his fist and put his knuckle near the door, only mere inches from the wooden opening in the house. Nature intensely watched as he moved his wrist backward and prepared for a series of three knocks—three loud, booming knocks—to wake the poor woman from her presumed sleep and bring her downstairs to alert her about the state of her dog.

CHAPTER X

Three loud knocks, a second in between, boomed on the door. Assuming that they should wait for the woman to come downstairs, they did, but they noticed that the door was hanging open, and the power of the three knocks pushed the door further. The youngest boy turned around slowly, eyes widened, mouth agape, eyebrows slanted in a face of fear, looking for encouragement from each of the boys and the girl. What had they done? The door was now open—unlocked—and they were standing right there.

"I suggest we walk inside," said the eldest Ledger boy.

"Are you crazy? No," said Andra.

"Well, look at the lock here. It must've been blown off by some brute force," said the eldest in retortion. As he talked, he turned to face each of the kids there, attempting to address the entire audience and gather support for his idea. "If the lock is broken, that means that something must have broken it, which means something entered the house, which means something could have harmed Ms. Kabila. I feel like, maybe, if we enter ourselves inside and perhaps just take a look around the area and determine if Ms. Kabila is ok, then we can secure ourselves, and it won't be a worry to us any further than this." There was silence for a few moments before he continued. "I mean, seriously, look at the lock! It isn't fallen or accidental—it is crushed and brutalized." The lock was truly broken off, perhaps by something like a hammer or a bullet that can easily ravage through the wood. It was evident she was broken into, and each of them seemed to infer that.

"Well, I am staying put right here. If you are crazy enough to trespass into the oldest woman's house in the neighborhood, which I know you were trying to say by using all that round-a-bout language by the way, then go right ahead. For what we know, the lock might just be broken!" explained Andra, clearly agitated by the boy's ideas.

"I don't know about this. It seems really sketchy," said the youngest boy again. "I am quite scared."

"Don't you want to see if she is good? She could be gone and that's why the dog is out," answered the eldest again. There was a dragged-out silence until someone else answered him.

"Yes. He has a point. I do agree with him, Andra. Let's just see if she is even here," said one of the Ledgers.

Andra looked deeply at each of them and let out a regrettable sigh, rolling her eyes at the thought of what she was about to say. "Alright, I guess we should go. Don't steal anything! I barely know you guys, and I don't want to be surrounded by, or worse, associated with fools."

Each of them stepped into the woman's house, looking closely at the furniture and the walls as if to see if the woman could be peering at them behind something. They were all hesitant to be intruding like this. There was something eerie about the situation, considering how quiet everything was. Nothing was moving or making noise save the boys, Andra, and the neglected dog.

Andra followed the dog upstairs towards the master bedroom. The dog stopped at the door, sitting and looking up at the girl with the hope that she would understand what he wants: to open the door. She pushed against it slightly, the rest of the movement caused by the dog itself as it ran its small body between the small crack. It walked behind the door toward the rest of the room, invisible to Andra at that moment.

On the bed lay Ms. Kabila, her face being licked by the dog who was lying next to her. She had evidently been shot multiple times in the stomach; a small puddle of blood made on the floor from the dribble of her wounds. She lay there, pale, as if the life previously within her had been sucked out and left in a state of torture.

Andra screamed. The boys quickly ran upstairs to her in an alarming state. She stood there, her palms on her eyes as her fingers spread and convulsed through her hair and on her smooth and beautiful skin. The boys looked at the sight, each of them gasping for air when they individually saw what was inside.

There was only lamplight giving life in the room. Each of them stood in front of the door, absorbing what was being seen. It was as if the buzz of the light was taunting them, making the noise of the calm while they shocked themselves with the fright of seeing a person so beloved, dead. The room was very well organized and was typical of an elderly woman's bedroom. Only the pillows on the bed, the bedsheets, and Ms. Kabila herself were any part disheveled.

"D-d-dead! —She is dead! Dead! —M-Ms. Kabila is dead!" screeched the young girl, shaking violently. She had begun screaming again, the same as she did when she was in agonizing pain about her ankle.

"Oh my—oh, God—we need to leave," said the eldest brother in a calm, demanding tone.

The younger brothers were hyperventilating at the sight, seemingly stuck in a frozen position. They had never seen a dead person before—none of them have. It shocked them to see someone walking around with such an effervescent and bubbly personality—loved especially by Andra's mother—indescribably unalive. After a small nudge, the boys began motioning backward and walked down the stairs. The eldest and second eldest Ledger helped the young girl go downstairs the same way they did when she was walking toward the house.

Once they were finally out of the house, they composed themselves, took deep breaths, and figured out what they needed to do next, for they had just discovered a dead woman! However, once they looked out onto the road, they noticed a small light moving very quickly. The teacup poodle made its way between the Ledger boy's legs and began howling in anger at the light, which now seemed to be moving toward them.

"What is that? Is it coming toward—us?" asked Andra, who was still sniffling at what she had just seen. After much squinting and focusing, they noticed it was the reflection of the wrist of a human being, presumably a watch, and it was on the wrist of a human being who was running. This human being began to call out, frightening the children evermore.

"You wretched children! Get over here now! What are you doing, breaking inside that woman's house? I saw you do it! I saw it when I was running with my dog. You get yourselves standing where I am at this moment, or else I will come to you." yelled what seemed to be a large, fast Russian man.

"Popov! Run!" said the eldest boy. Each of the children sprinted around the side of the house, except for Andra, who was hindered by her devastated ankle. She attempted to hobble in the same direction as the boys and constantly looked back to see the silhouette of the man pacing quicker than her. Every few steps, she felt like the Russian was closer to her, and once she saw that he was only twenty feet from her, she fell to the ground and rolled slightly, screaming in fear.

"Boys! Wait!" she wailed loudly. Against her fortune, they did not wait and continued to hurry in the direction of their home without turning back to make sure she was safe. Once the boys had disappeared along the road, she could hear the footsteps directly behind her, approaching ever so fast.

"Stop moving!" insisted Popov, as he grabbed her from behind, interlocking his fingers so she could not escape his grip. She could hear the echoes of the warning her brother had given her earlier, and how she felt he was going to kill her, just like his last victims. "You aren't going anywhere until the police arrive. I don't tolerate crime in this neighborhood," said the Russian man.

"Let go of me! I am crippled, and you are taking advantage of it! Let go, let go, let go!" ordered Andra, scrambling to get off the man and back on her feet to go home.

"No. I am keeping you here until the police arrive. I already alerted them. Don't think I wasn't watching you all from behind and witnessing you choose the decision to walk inside that house. You contemplated it, discussed it, and still chose to trespass! What were you trying to steal, huh?" he asked, enraged at her resistance.

"We weren't stealing! We tried to return her lost dog! It was barking, I know you hear that at least. Let me go!" said she, elbowing him in the stomach.

It didn't faze him in the slightest, and he might as well have tightened his grip. Her screams had awoken most of the neighbors from their sleep, and it wasn't long until the rest of her family had been alerted too.

❋   ❋   ❋

The police arrived at the scene. They kindly asked the Russian to relieve the girl of his grip, and he did so accordingly. Behind them, a surge of neighbors made a considerable audience as they saw what happened. They talked about what was going on and made a substantial gossip, which spread into each ear and was regurgitated out of each mouth, mutated slightly as to become a wilder and spicier gossip.

Standing in the crowd was Lady Farrow, who was alongside each of her biological children who stared directly ahead at Cassandra Shabah. One of the children had a particularly concerned face, unlike the rest of them. Lady Farrow rubbed their shoulders, hoping to relax them. Rushing down the road towards the crows was also Ms. Shabah, who seemed muddled at the sight of her daughter, an old man, and the cops. As she arrived, the Farrows immediately left.

Ms. Shabah's first thought was that there was some sexual affair occurring. She knew that her daughter was significantly attractive and observable beautiful, attracting men and women alike. However, she was quickly mistaken once she heard talk about how the girl is a child murderer and the old man had found her.

"I suggest you lot shut your mouths! How dare you—being at the ripe age that you are—talk about someone who is not even sixteen! You foul lot! Go to bed before you die in your wrinkly skin!" announced Ms. Shabah. The crowd quieted, and after only a few minutes, dispersed. Ms. Shabah believed that she embarrassed the crowd well enough that they had to leave.

Ms. Shabah was the only person left at the scene; Gabriel was nowhere to be found. He did not bother leaving the house, although Ms. Shabah did not remember seeing him. The police began to question the girl, and Ms. Shabah listened intently.

"Why are you here?"

"I told you; I was here with those Ledger boys. They dragged me along with them to find her to talk about her dogs—and she—was dead! I—I found her like that. There was no ill harm intended—I have a broken ankle; I can barely walk!"

"We understand, but it doesn't make sense why you would run from Mr. Popov. He clearly had no ill intent, but *you* ran."

"Yes, I ran because he was chasing me! I believe that is ill intent. If he was the person who had killed this woman, why would I have stayed? There was only a matter of time before he got me."

"I saw her, sir! I saw the whole lot leave the house in a hurry. I even saw them enter, right before I made my way over there. She killed her, alright, she killed her!" exclaimed Popov in the background, clearly listening to the conversation.

"Sir, I do not need your articulation of the events that occurred. I will talk to you separately. It seems as if you stumbled upon the late Ms. Kabila, and that this entire case has been blown out of proportion because of an overwhelming sense of sadness. This has been a large misunderstanding. Cassandra, I am going to have to bring you into a formal office for questioning soon. This will be furthered later. I will fax or mail a letter with the exact information. Since you are so young, and this case was because of a trespassing problem originally, I am allowing you to be temporarily free to go."

"Thank you, sir. I appreciate it. Do not let that man go without questioning him, however. He had run quite fast to get me. I am a mere cripple!" said Andra, in return. The police gave her a piece of paper detailing each of the processes of how the mail will be received, when to go into questioning as a witness, and how the future will look for her and this case that has opened. He was surprisingly calm throughout the process—something that the Shabah family thought was odd considering how heavy and serious the police were with something as extraordinary and unusual as a murder case.

Once she received the piece of paper, she ran back to her mother, who was crying hysterically at the sight of seeing her daughter with the police. They warmly embraced. Ms. Shabah immediately began talking about what had happened, curious and distressed as to what this sight meant.

"What has happened, Cassandra? What were they talking about with some woman dead? Why are you involved in this whatsoever?" asked Cassandra's mother, nervous for whatever answer the Shabah girl was going to reply.

"Mother," she began as she started to tear up, "I do not know any other way I can say this, but—something terrible has happened. Happened to—Ms. Kabila. She is—dead. She died in her house, and I went to investigate because of something completely separate. I found her dog astray—covered in mud—and I wanted to let her know that I found it and that it was safe now. I was with those Ledger boys—they wanted me to come with them; we were going to ask her if she was abusive. I found her after that," said the girl, in a low pitch, attempting to muffle what she had said to make its impact lesser.

Ms. Shabah did not say another word. She solely wept at what she had just heard. Ms. Kabila was one of the kindest women she had ever met, and whenever she saw her, it was as if a fresh breath of air was available to breathe, and as if the sunshine was able to light a dark room. It was as if a vacuum had cleaned the dust off her dark life, and a rejuvenation occurred. Ms. Shabah was devastated. The poor woman who had been the most tenderhearted person to reveal themselves in the neighborhood had passed away, leaving her and her family stranded in a toxic waste controlled by the Farrow household.

Once she had arrived home, still weeping with Cassandra, they found a note at their front step. It was short and quickly written, but its effect was powerful, and not in a good way.

62

Dearest residents,
A child murderer of one of our best and brightest. How disgusting. I hope they realize how their terrorization does not scare us. If the Shabah can see this, leave! We do not want you or your child felons.

Carol Farrow

Ms. Shabah took the note and a small instrument from her cabinet. "Wait here," she uttered to the young Cassandra. She walked out of her home and stood directly in front of the Farrow house. In her hand was a lighter and the note that was given to her. She saw in the window that there was a woman and three other heads peering through the darkness. Ms. Shabah lit the note on fire, dropped it on the ground, and walked away.

For the rest of the night, Cassandra Shabah and Ms. Shabah slept in the same bed together, mourning the death of the beloved woman who had treated them far beyond what anyone else has. Ms. Kabila made an effort, and unlike the rest of the neighbors here in Quintbridge, she was serious about protecting new neighbors. She had known what it was like to be thrown into an environment where she was not liked, and so the Shabah family felt like something similar. That is why she cared for them so much.

Ms. Shabah felt alone here, and now that Cassandra had been dragged into a murder case, she felt ashamed to have decided to move here. The only thing she could do without any trouble possibly occurring is sleep, and that is exactly what she intended to do. Within a few short minutes, she and Cassandra were sleeping, still grasping each other passionately in the bed of a pink room with small animals lining the walls. It was quiet and serene, perfectly sound and comfortable; they were together, a family, which is all that there could be that is reliable in the end.

CHAPTER XI

Once the crowd stopped wailing, and all that remained were the Russian, the Shabah, and the investigator, Gabriel stepped foot outside, into the brisk and enlivening air of Quintbridge. He had known what had happened to his sister, and now that his mother was gone to go observe the situation, he took some time to evaluate his thoughts.

"Oh, this is the most terrible situation! My poor sister! This neighborhood—I cannot deal with it any longer. How this has become such a distraction to our living and adjusting is incredibly frustrating! I am not sure how I am supposed to just sit in this gloomy house, acting as if everything is OK. It isn't!" he thought to himself. There was a deeper issue that Gabriel hadn't realized yet—his anxieties and overwhelming emotions flooded within him. There was an overflow of thoughts that he could not control. "I know what to do. I need a break from this area. I must go! I have to leave before anyone has a chance to persuade me otherwise!" thought Gabriel.

He walked back upstairs to his bedroom, where underneath his bed were a variety of small bags and cases to store things inside. He pulled out one of his oldest—a grey bag from his kindergarten days in Fiddlefield. He remembered when he used to walk through the botanical gardens with this bag, fidgeting with the orange whistle that hung low and watching the rose bushes shake and wisp around while the wind timidly bestowed its force upon them. He remembered his last use with the bag, where he pulled out a leather-bound journal in the same Fiddlefield forest where he had always written, and wrote a short, prosaic passage about the log he sat upon and its history—how it had gotten to where it lay. He found a caterpillar climbing on the side of the bag and decided it was infested, and he never used it again.

Now, he pulled his trusty bag back from underneath his bed and filled it with a few things he might need. His primary journal, a blank journal, six pens in case all five previous ones manage to break or dry, a bottle of water, and some apples wrapped in tissues so they would not get dirty. He packed each of them carefully while in a frantic mood, believing his life to be too overwhelming for him to live through. A small note about his whereabouts was left on his bed, making it known that he would only be gone for a short time before he returned, revitalized like a metal wire struck by lightning. He knew that his sister and mother would be too distraught to go check on him in his room, but he left it there anyway, just in case.

He put on his sandals and headed outside in the night. Ahead of him, the three biological Farrow children were carrying buckets filled with slips of paper, which he naturally assumed were notes from the dreadful Lady Farrow. He ignored them, however, and made his way left of his house, away from the Ledgers and the catastrophe involving his family and the police. Gabriel was aware of the shape of the neighborhood, where the roads led in an oval shape. It did not matter which way he turned, for he was always going to end up at the same destination. The only difference was that if he turned to the right, he would be able to go where he wanted quicker, but, wanting to avoid the nuisance that was the police and his family and their situation, he turned left.

He walked past the Lillis house, where Cassandra Farrow was probably staying—hiding from her mother—and he stopped there for a moment. He argued in his mind. Would it be better to completely pass their house and go somewhere else, or should he knock to see if Cassandra wanted to see him? Should he also stay with Cassandra Farrow, if the Lillis twins permit it, or should he go back home? There was a feeling of longing for her; he missed her dearly. He wasn't sure why, for he did not like her in the beginning, as did his sister. However, she was the only person always willing to make themselves available to him.

Was Cassandra someone who had a particular liking for him? He noticed that she yearned to be around him—wanting his presence, needing it—but he never fully digested what that could have meant. Did he miss her and the journeys they made around the neighborhood together, like that of the sisters in Little Women, or did he miss the love she exuded to him, like Catherine and Heathcliff, inseparable while they terrorized their home and the moors? He decided to leave, not wanting to see her until she was ready to see him.

Instead, he continued along his path, hoping to encounter someplace where he could stay, and before long, a place like such was made available. The red peonies hidden within the garden of the house were not unnoticeable, along with the small marks on each side of the door and grazes on some parts of the walls on the exterior: the house where his beauty Delilah Candella lived was inviting him. He quickly approached the front door and knocked four times, the first one unnecessarily hard while the latter was much softer. At this untimely hour, he realized that no one was likely to open the door. He made himself feel like an idiot.

"Hello? Who is this?" asked the person from the other side of the door. It was the unique voice of the lovely girl that had been gifted the heart of Gabriel.

"Hello, Delilah. Oh, thank you for answering! Or at least being awake! I'm so sorry for possibly waking you at this hour—I know it is late. Could you please open the door? I am desperate to tell you some things," said he, both excitedly but with a tang of nervousness that trembled his voice. The sounds he made from his throat cracked after every few seconds—an after-effect of his crying.

There was a moment of hesitation before the door creaked open, revealing the stunning Delilah. She looked at him concerningly, but not out of care. It was more like that of someone who is crazily knocking at their door in the night, possibly high on drugs. "What do you want, Gabriel?"

"I know this favor is large, but I must ask you. I have no one else to ask—"

"Spit it out!"

"Alright. May I sleep here for the night? I am so overwhelmed at my own home. I have neither Cassandra to talk to. My sister is in trouble with the police and Cassandra Farrow is in hiding, or at least I believe she is. I have no one to console me. Will you?"

She looked at him with an expression that seemed like she didn't care for what he asked. However, she acquiesced. "Sure, you may. Come inside, but do not make a noise. If I am caught with an unknown guest in my house—let alone my room—I will be executed by my parents. You don't understand how they treat me! Don't think I am getting abused, by the way, because I am being sarcastic. I'm just joking. You probably knew that. Come along!" she said.

They entered her room. The first thing Gabriel noticed was the abundance of red. There were red curtains, a red sofa, red pillows, and a red tapestry hanging on her wall. Spanish posters were on each wall, some large, some small, and they were surrounded by other paintings that were completely original—presumably the paintings of Delilah herself. Inspirational quotes in Spanish were above her bed frame and below each poster, also written in red writing. A magnificent bookshelf—entirely full—was near her desk, filled with some of the greatest classics in literature like Don Quijote de la Mancha, Moby Dick, Middlemarch, the entire collection of the Brontë sister's novels, and other books of grand scope, like every volume of Jane Austen's Emma and Persuasion. She seemed to have a thing for satire. Her small desk had a large husk of an animal, presumably used by her to study anatomical differences and similarities, as well as something of a notepad with detailed sketches and paragraphs of information.

There were stacks of magazines and textbooks, mixed with each other, an easel in the corner, empty and half-finished canvases on the floors, and clothes spread out everywhere. There was enough clean space to make room for the boy to sleep, so she put some sheets and one of her many pillows on the ground, attempting to make a comfortable space there.

"Here—I put this together, it's the best I can do. If you need anything else, let me know. I must set my alarm a little earlier so you can leave without being found by my parents. I cannot have you getting me in trouble—not now at least. Anyways, why are you here?" she said in the softest voice. It was like a Goldfinch was talking to him, seducing him with the song of love that easily left her parted lips. Her eyes glistened with the beams of moonlight that came from her window and with the lamps of red stained-glass bottles that she seemed to make herself from wax, a lightbulb, and a bottle of presumably Coca-Cola, mesmerizing viewers with the rise and fall of the wax.

"I—don't know. I just need a break from living at my place. There is something terribly wrong with the Farrow family, you know. They have been spreading letters around about us for weeks now, and I don't know how much they expect me to take. You are honestly beauti—I mean *easy* to talk to, considering how we met the first time," he said, tripping on each of his words as if he could not formulate any sentences.

"I'm not sure where you got that inference from. We met once, Gabriel. It was such a hurry too. Maybe you should figure out what the exact reason for you coming here is. It seems strange to me that you pop over here to sleep over, in the middle of the night, and now can't explain yourself exactly. You just told me you don't know, and then something about letters, and know how easy I am to talk to. It seems odd," said the young girl. She sat on her bedsheets in her pajamas, comfortable and cozy in her personalized room. Gabriel felt uneasy intruding in her home like this, but also thrilled to now be in the same vicinity with Delilah, which he longed for so badly!

"Never mind about that, Delilah. I will have to tell you another time—when I am more level-headed. What are you doing awake at this hour, though? Do tell me," said he. She moved toward a large photo album next to her bed, holding it back up to her face. Her soft skin caressed each page with care and delicacy—a radiance flowed within that girl.

"I was researching some art that is going to be in an exhibition in the next few weeks—all Spanish art—and reading all the small paragraphs that are attached with each piece. This exhibition released what they are showcasing early, and so I get to read all the meaningful paragraphs that the artists write themselves in advance—mostly so that when I view the art itself, I can appreciate it better. Did you know I used to be an artist myself? Since I was eleven years old, I used to paint pictures of things I see or ideas that I would have, and I would sell them; some people paid very good money for these pieces—even ranging up to a thousand dollars. When I go to college, I hope it will be easier to pay since I have stored most of it in savings, but occasionally my parents need some money, so I give them some."

"Are each of the paragraphs in Spanish?"

"Yes, they are."

"Oh, I wish I could read them. I know almost no Spanish apart from the common 'Hola,'"

"Well, that seems like quite a problem," said she, laughing quietly. It made Gabriel blush when he heard her whistling laugh cascade through his ears.

"Maybe you could teach me?" he asked. She paused for a moment, testing to see if he was serious about his question. When she saw his uneasy facial expression, she realized that he indeed was.

"Sure, I can. It is a whole new language, though, so it will take many months, possibly multiple years, to get to the same level I am at. You won't learn enough in time!"

"Oh, I don't care. I just want to hear your voice while you teach me, and I will learn very quickly. I am intent on listening to you, Delilah."

Her cheeks flushed pink, and she turned to the side, avoiding his gaze. She gave in, however, and promised that she would teach the young boy everything there is to know about the Spanish language in the best way she could.

Gabriel had never been so careful with his words; everything he said was with caution and care, making sure not to accidentally offend her or turn her against him with some polarizing idea he had accidentally released. Delilah seemed keen on getting to know Gabriel on a deeper level, examining his intellect and his emotional intelligence. She wanted to know more about him, and she could not help herself from asking him questions. 'Have you had a girlfriend? What is your favorite color? Why did you move here? Where exactly is Fiddlefield in the scope of the nation? Are you enrolled in the same school as me?' The plethora of questions was answered just as enthusiastically as they were asked, and every time, Gabriel returned the question to her, asking her the same, so he could gather an identical amount of information. He desperately wanted to take out his journal to take notes on each of her responses but felt as if that would make her uncomfortable.

All night the two lay together, talking about superficial get-to-know-me questions and debating what color mathematics should represent and why art is a means of societal expression rather than making something look incredible. Afterward, they practiced some basic Spanish rules and covered a few verbs that were common in conversational Spanish. Gabriel no longer felt the pessimism that tormented him for all the time before—it was as if the girl had swallowed and digested it away into a waste—and Delilah felt as if he was a needed break from the familial responsibilities she held each day.

CHAPTER XII

When they looked outside and noticed they could see the leaves of the trees without the need for a light, they decided it would be a good time for Gabriel to go back home. He left his house so he could sleep there but stayed awake the entire night, defeating his original expectation at the fault of his own heart. Originally, Gabriel was conflicted as to whether he enjoyed the presence of the exquisite Delilah Candella more than that of the scattered Cassandra Farrow—two neighborly best friends—and could not decide if he wanted to allow himself to love them, but after a night of conversation with Delilah, he made sure of it. Delilah was the girl he had been waiting for—the subconscious reason for moving to this town. Gabriel thought the Gods above him aligned the two together on purpose, believing that their love was perfect for each other; a dynamic duo like shoes and socks, salt and pepper, wheel and wagon.

He and Delilah walked through the house sneakily, passing each of the random assortment of toys and ignoring the holes and paint scratches on all the walls until they got to the front door. They opened the door as quietly as they could, hoping that the noise would be so subtle as to keep her family asleep.

"Well—would you look at this—it is day outside and we got no sleep! You kept me awake with your intriguing questions and answers. I regret talking to you," she said with a smile.

"I don't regret anything. I found you interesting beyond regular levels, Lila. May I begin to call you Lila?"

"Sure, if that pleases you. I thought Delilah was a beautiful name—I have always had pride in it—but if you feel that Lila is better, you may call me that."

"I do think Delilah is a good name, but I think Lila is a more personal—for me."

"Well then it is settled—Lila you shall call me. I am sure it will grow on me eventually, but I have never experienced a nickname. Everyone has always called me Delilah. Anyways, I think I am going to get started on making some coffee for the rest of the day."

"If my mother allows it, I can bring you a mug with some coffee. The farmer's market just imported some coffee beans from Colombia, which we heard was quite an interesting taste—in a good way. If I bring some to you, will you go on a walk around the neighborhood this morning? Perhaps we could even go to the farmer's market to see the beans from South America."

"Sounds good. I will have to do a few chores before I leave. After that, I should be good to leave, and I can meet you at your house. Make me two coffees, please. I need to stay awake for the rest of the day, and I feel incredibly drowsy."

"Claro que sí. Hasta luego," said Gabriel in his broken Spanish accent that he received from one sleepy night's practice.

"Chao, Gabriel," she returned.

When she went back inside, softly closing the front door of her home, Gabriel made his way back home. It was difficult to keep his eyes open, but he felt more alive and aware than he had ever felt. It was a strange feeling to be as tired as he was—sensitive to noise just as much as his brain muffled the noises to put him safely to sleep. Yet, he heard the calls of the birds above, so clearly conversing from trees and the branches to each other. They were all differently sounding, some a small whistle, some a high-pitched scream, and some even a bellowing squawk, and he wondered if it was even possible to picture how many different birds existed in this environment.

Humans failed to take notice of the environment that coexists among them in patterns and realities just as complex as their own. Gabriel was beginning to take notice: the same cool breeze that lessened the radiating heat of the sun; the calls of the birds that gave sound and substance to the otherwise quiet and dead air; the trees that probably took thousands of years from nothing to expand into the level of expanse that it was currently in, and their shading leaves that moved freely through the air; even the hundreds of tons of water that lay flat in the small crater in the ground that had somehow appeared in the years before, housing some beautiful fish that cruised in the waters, searching for food or fleeing the predator. It was an epiphany he began to experience, resulting from the misty mind that he had from his lack of sleep.

He realized that he had finally arrived back at his house, where no lights were turned on—by candle or by bulb—and that the surrounding houses were just as silent. He wondered at what time he was arriving. At once, he entered his house and found the clock to tell the time as 6 a.m., and he had figured his mother and sister were still asleep. He had set the teapot on a warm fire, to which it immediately began to boil, and made himself two mugs of coffee—one for himself and one for Delilah Candella, which he was so excited to see once again.

He then sat down on his desk and pulled out a small slip of paper on which he wrote his plans for the day. "I am outside with Delilah, the girl from the neighborhood which I am beginning to like a lot more and will be home soon after that. I took two mugs of coffee with me to bring to her since it is quite early. I hope you are all feeling better," he wrote. He felt more kind to have said a happy sentiment to them, which he has not said before, and he left the note next to the teapot, where he knew his mother would find it when she went to make her coffee for the morning.

As he made his way back outside, stinging his tongue with the feeling of the hot coffee swishing in his mouth, he once again felt the same notice of the environment and made a mental note to bring it up to Delilah when he saw her again. However, he could not find her at the agreed meeting place, and made his way toward her house, thinking that perhaps the tasks she needed to do might have taken longer than expected.

Soon enough, they met each other in the middle, both walking toward each other like two tired folks. He handed her the mug, now only warm, not hot like it was before, and she sipped it with delight, brightening and becoming more enlivened with each swig of the South American mixture.

"Nice to see you," said Gabriel sarcastically.

"Likewise. It has been *so* long. This coffee is quite delicious and definitely wakes me up for the rest of the day. Come with me," she said as she continued to sip the delicious brown drink. The two walked side-by-side, talking about nonsense, the origins of the coffee they drank, the rest of the neighborhood, and the case of Cassandra and Ms. Kabila. It was quite shocking to Delilah, who believed that Popov was at fault because of his rumored history, but she did not say anything about that. She did not want to tell him her opinions, because she did not want him to perceive her as nosy and melodramatic.

"This weather here is unlike anything I have ever experienced. People believe that talking about the weather is mundane and boring, useless and an impractical conversation starter. But the weather is fascinating. The physical reactions of the human body are dictated by

72

the weather, something that only Mother Nature can control herself. Have you the weather that was necessary for creating the beans that your coffee was brewed with? The hot, tropical weather of Colombia, so strong and powerful in its influence, created the perfect sip of coffee to wake you from a tired state. Have you considered the breeze that plagues this incredibly cool and beautiful neighborhood, and how it is formed and continues to be formed until, probably, time ends? These are the thoughts I think of every day, Lila. Now, I am given a new thought—your life. It is you that I can place my abstract and deep thoughts into focus on, and you that I can consider the state and the effect of. Have you considered any thoughts like these?" asked the boy so carefully quiet and precise with his words.

"Yes, I actually have thought about those. I do consider the weather occasionally, but my larger and more focused thoughts occur with the history and the voice. I enjoy thinking about the speaking a president or a royal member does to provoke an audience, the historical context of paintings like those that will be featured in the upcoming exhibit in town, and even the combinations of the two. It has always been my dream to successfully work within the law, and I have strived toward that goal my whole life. It has grasped the entirety of my thoughts: the *absolute* entirety. Only last night did I begin to think of you because the awkward and unimportant encounter we had with Cassandra Farrow was of no significance to me. When you left, I began to imagine your movements as you created this masterpiece of a coffee, and I imagined all the movements of your hair, and I thought about how you would talk to your mother and your sister, and everything else in between—solely about you. I now think about something else—it is preoccupying me so terribly—but what have I replaced in my thoughts to now think of you? Everything I have ever thought and planned and experienced in my mind was the same thing, and I had no space to consider anything else. Yet now you are in there. It is scary and wonderful how vulnerable I have become because of you, all at the same time."

They both went quiet for a few moments, passing by the pond as they watched a few storks fly by. They watched as the green trees swished in the constant breeze, and how the small opening in between the trees, where a few logs stood proudly, remained stoic and silent. However, in the distance, a couple of Irishmen marched their way towards them, both at the brave age of eight and turned and twisted as they ran past, wearing the same clothes as they had the first time Gabriel had ever seen them: the same red flannel short pants and the blue and green shirts with no other designs on them. They curiously walked past Delilah and Gabriel as they made their trek toward the pond.

"Hey! You two! Come over here, I must ask you something," said Gabriel boldly. The two boys wandered over, laughing and giggling at the sight of Gabriel acting so manly and masculine. They were dizzy with humor and goofiness, walking around without staying in place like they had been instructed.

"What do ya' wanna know? We could probably help ya' both," said one of the identical twins.

"When are we going to be able to see Cassandra again? Everyone knows that you two rascals have her locked away in your house, and we all want to see her again. Actually, we want to know what happened to her and how she is going to come back to us more importantly," said Gabriel

"I thought ya' mother di'n' want ya' to be gossipy. She said she hates a good gossip, right Connor?" asked one twin to the other.

"That is very right, Cormac, very right indeed," said the other twin.

"I don't care what either of you has to say, we must know when and where we could find her. It is urgent and you are being unhelpful," said Gabriel.

"If you don't tell us, we are going to break your little ankles with our bare hands and you will never walk these streets again, and if that does not work and we find you walking, we will use something more brutal," said Delilah sternly. "Do you want the same thing to happen to you as last time?"

"No! We will tell you!" said the twins at the same time. It seems clear that Delilah had done something to them in the past because they stopped moving around in circles like zombified idiots and stood scared, eyebrows turned downwards like the basic image of a sad boy. One of the twins continued. "We think you could find Cassandra at the pond by the logs right there—she usually likes to sit and scrapbook in her papers. Sometimes she does that calicus stuff she always works on, too. Around sunset. Delilah, please don't hurt us!"

"I won't. And it is pronounced *cal-cue-lus*. Thank you, boys. Now scram!" she said in her soft voice before looking back up at Gabriel. She had a strange expression of rage that seemed artificial but then burst into a laugh as she realized how ridiculous she is. "They think

I can murder them because they witnessed me disciplining my siblings. I find it hilarious."

"You're just too intimidating. Anyways, I think I better go back home, my mother is probably awake, and I am in desperation for some of her home-cooked eggs. Would you like to join and spend the rest of the day with me?" he asked kindly.

"No, I think I couldn't. I already know the list of things to do is getting increasingly long. However, it is only Wednesday, and the art exhibit is on Friday. If you could join me on that, I would appreciate it. It is early in the morning, and I don't take you as a morning person, so if it is too much of a challenge—"

"No! It is not a challenge! I can make it a priority to wake up that morning. Have no doubts, Lila, I will come with you!"

"Lovely. I will talk to you later. Goodbye for now!"

"Bye! I hope to see you again soon!" he said. Delilah laughed and handed him his mug back. She turned away, walking down the same strip of road that Gabriel had when he went on his search for sleep yesternight. On his way back, when he saw his house in view, he scarcely saw two curious heads bobbing up and down behind the hill in the driveway.

At first glance, it seemed to him that the twins were ravaging through the trash like he had been warned of by the lovely Cassandra Farrow. However, on a second glance, he managed to see that the heads had hair that seemed more blonde than red, something that was more curious to him than anything else he had seen yet in this neighborhood.

CHAPTER XIII

Gabriel managed to find a way to sneak through the trees to get the best look possible and saw that it was no one other than his next-door neighbors, the Victorianas.

In the trash was the woman, foraging for something so desperately, and looking through the cracks of the driveway was the man. Both residents were known to be the richest and most perfect examples of success that Quintbridge had to offer, and yet here they were, in their most vulnerable moments, scavenging for something in their neighbor's driveway.

"Excuse me! What are you doing?" yelled Gabriel, looking confused and concerned. The two looked up from their search, seeming equally terrified and anxious. They looked at each other, and their eyes reddened and swelled with tears that were soon to come. The lady started to hyperventilate, while the man looked directly at the boy, seeming intimidated by the boy's presence there. "Are you going to answer me, or are you going to keep looking for something in the driveway of my home?" A shrill was emitted from the woman, as she covered her mouth with her dirty palms, looking at her husband in fear. They remained silent. "Stay right here, I am going to get my mother. If you move, I will find you, and make this situation much worse than it currently is. Disgusting thieves," he muttered and jogged inside to fetch his mother so she could take charge of the situation.

A few tears began to roll down the eyes of lady Victoriana. Her husband seemed in a state of shock and did not know what to do with himself and herself. They were petrified of what Ms. Shabah would say to them, and how they would be treated if she decided to tell everyone else in the neighborhood; they had already had a hard time since the recent news. For the moments that the Shabah family was not present, the Victoriana couple had a glimpse of hope that they would take pity on them, allowing them to have some money to restart their life or give them food to eat while they prayed this terrible period of time would disappear. However, it quickly diminished when they realized the situation they were in. They were scouring for something to eat in the trash of their next-door neighbor, looking for pennies hidden within the cracks of the driveway concrete, and anything that was accidentally misplaced by the Shabahs that they could find value in to sell for money. At once, Ms. Shabah and her children walked out of the house, concerned and angry.

"What in God's name are you doing? Why are you in my trash? I see your hands covered in the smelly liquids of my waste. I don't even know both of your first names, and this is how you are treating my house? You better explain yourselves," said the woman in her strictest voice.

The lady began to cry, and the man held her close, warming her with his rubs on her arm. "Well, my name is Florence, and my husband's name is Granger. We were... oh! It is just too shameful to explain," she said, breaking into a fit of tears. "We are so poor, so very poor! We needed something to eat, and we wanted to find something—anything—that had value so we can sell it. We were so desperate for something to eat or something to sell that we went looking through the trash. Carol Farrow said that a commitment between all neighbors to never talk to us again, because we are so unfortunately poor and broke, is in full force, and no one will talk to us for the rest of our time here. We have nowhere to go, and no one to talk to about any of this, and it is all because we have no money. God! I am exhausted from having no money!" Ms. Shabah and her children felt sad for their misfortune but felt that what they had done—snooping through their waste and looking on their driveway for fallen coins—was unacceptable.

"The bank thought that we could not live there anymore—and we vowed not to use anything that could make us pay something, like lights, etcetera—but they did not listen to us, and they took our house away," continued Granger Victoriana, who was holding his wife while she sobbed into his shoulder. "They sold it to a pair of girls, who are the best of friends and have wanted to live here forever. We realized that we cannot go anywhere, because we are now homeless, and what are we to do without anywhere to stay? So, we decided we were going to inhabit the crawlspace under the house. We hear them having such a great time above us, dancing and laughing and eating, and all we can do is imagine that one day that will be us. We imagine that this is not real and that we are actually living our same lives again, except those imaginations are so easily diminished when we feel the rain or the heat of the outside. Look at the state of Florence's hair! It is like a disgusting rag—no offense meant by that, my dear—and it is so gross living out here. We apologize for looking through your trash, invading your privacy, and being the worst, most primitive citizens of this esteemed neighborhood. This place is ruining us, Shabahs, absolutely ruining us!"

As the couple was ranting about their current life situation, expressing every emotion they had ever felt, a young teenage boy, taller than Gabriel, began to walk by the house excessively fast. He took out a small black box—a Kodak camera—and took a snapshot of their situation. It had been quite peculiar because no one could properly recognize the boy. It was only until the boy smiled with his flagrant attitude and envious style that Ms. Shabah realized who it was: no other than the eldest biological Farrow child.

"Would you look at that! It is like we are the king of England, walking through the grounds of Quintbridge for all to see. It is like we are a preposterous group of people who cannot help but walk like they have a massive following of thousands of people behind them. How do people have the guts to take a photograph of all of us, just to ridicule us in front of the world?" said Granger Victoriana. Ms. Shabah nodded at him in agreement.

"Listen to me. I think that you need to just leave. We all know what is to come of that terrible photo, especially if it is the young Farrow boy like I perceived." The Victoriana couple bowed their head once they had heard the name, bringing the light to the face of the boy whose identity they had previously not known. "In my opinion, you both just need to leave. We certainly cannot help you, but in my opinion, the best investment you could have is a casino or a gambling house, or if you have any wealthy relatives or friends that could loan you money, ask them. Otherwise, you both have no business being here right now. Do not leave the neighborhood, though. There could always be an opportunity that arises out of the twisting smoke of this neighborhood. Stay where you are settled right now. As long as the two girls are at bay and stay busy, they won't find you or look for you. Have some confidence in yourselves, and I promise you that you will not die out here.

"May we have a hug, Ms. Shabah?" asked Florence.

"Of course, my dear." the two embraced, and then Ms. Shabah moved to Granger Victoriana, hugging him too. The couple then went over the fence between the driveway and the Victoriana's old home, where they snuggled under some rags and blankets beneath the home, barely in view unless someone concentrated very hard. Ms. Shabah told the children not to say a word to anyone about this, no matter how much the impulses within them ask to be free. They agreed to keep their tongue silent, and that there is no use in telling anyone because they aren't gossips, which made Ms. Shabah very proud of the way she raised her children. As they walked inside, Ms. Shabah heard some commotion from in front of her house. She hurried Gabriel and Cassandra inside and went outside to look for what was calling her attention.

"Hello, love! How have you been? What is going on at your house? I keep seeing people walking past seeming shocked or confused by what they are seeing, or someone who took a photo. Very interesting to me, so I thought I would come by and see what is going on," said Bonnie Grealm, the neighbor next door.

"Oh, well, Bonnie, I believe everything is very well over here. There is nothing going on worth troubling yourself over. What do you need?" asked Ms. Shabah

"Well, I have noticed that I haven't been receiving any letters from the Farrow woman. Have you been receiving anything?"

"No. I haven't ever received any. I used to read them when I went on walks with Ms. Kabila, but… well—never mind about that. I have never had the pleasure of being sent the most putrid descriptions of myself like the rest of the residents here. I must go inside and begin dinner—I was planning to make a large ham—so I better get going. Is there anything else you need to mention?"

"Not necessarily. I hope to see you around, then. Perhaps we could have some wine together one night just to wind down and talk about things and such," said Bonnie. Ms. Shabah focused deeply on the words she used, the 'talk about things,' and thought it was rather disgusting.

"Maybe we could figure something out. Nice to see you! Bye, lovely," said Ms. Shabah, and hurriedly walked inside her home. Bonnie seemed confused at the sudden urgency but disregarded it and began walking back home.

CHAPTER XIV

When the sun fell below the clouds and painted the wisps of white a cool orange color, and when the breeze of the night was in the very beginnings of whistling through the leaves of the trees, Gabriel decided to go outside and go towards the pond, where he was in hopes of finding Cassandra. He asked his sister if she would like to come along, and she quickly agreed. "Oh, I haven't been out of the house in ages, and I would love to go!" She hadn't left in fear of seeing the Russian man once again, who had attempted on framing her for murder.

The investigation of Ms. Kabila was not going anywhere. It had been days since the police were back in the neighborhood. Andra went into questioning, where she answered a small series of questions with boring and unimportant answers, leaving the police puzzled as to who it could be that committed such a crime. There were no motives to be found, and since Ms. Kabila lived a reserved and solitary life in her estate, the only people she interacted with had no malicious intent swimming within their bodies. Cassandra was afraid that Popov would attempt to regain the police's attention on herself once again, and that was the last thing she needed. Running from the man had terribly pushed back her progress on healing her ankle—she had originally been expected to heal within a couple of months, but it was like she had broken her ankle again and was now expected to completely heal in the middle of July. Her first time coming out of the house in many days was to be tonight when she hoped she could see Jason.

At the peak of the sunset, where the colors were most saturated and the light seemed brighter than a few moments before, the two Shabah siblings went outside and found themselves trekking between the trees where the house of the neighbor next to Lady Farrow stood. The forests were dense, as were all the forests in Quintbridge, but this forest, in particular, was unnecessarily bushy and full of extending twigs and branches among the thorn bushes and husks of rotting wood found throughout this area. After a few minutes of pushing through leaves that poked and scratched against their skin, they made it to a small clearing where they could see the miniature ripples of the pond tapping against the stones and jutting topography.

At the pond's edge, close to the same group of logs that Gabriel had seen earlier when he was with Delilah Candella, were the Ledger boys, fishing with a small line and a handmade bait. They stood together talking, while the youngest threw the line out and intermittently pulled it back in, appearing to create an illusion of a small fish to attract larger fish. It was not successful, but he persisted. The Shabah Siblings walked over to them, stepping in the small patches of moss and balancing over the smooth stones that lined the pond.

"Hello, Ledgers. What are you doing out here this fine sunset?" asked Cassandra Shabah.

"Oh my, Andra! I have not seen you in so long! It is so nice to see your familiar face, so kind and smooth in this light, once again," said the eldest. The other boys also were excited and said some small comments about her appearance.

"Well, it is nice to see you all also, but you have not answered my question. Why are you guys here?" she asked once again.

"We came here to fish. It is calming to fish on a sunset like this."

"I see that. It is quite mesmerizing to watch the bait reel in like that."

"Yes, we agree. Why are you two here at this hour? I don't see any drinks or fishing materials on you."

"We are here because of a word by the Lillis twins," said Gabriel, answering the question in place of his sister. "When I was walking with Delilah Candella, we saw them roaming about, as they usually do, and we asked them where we could find Cassandra Farrow since we have not seen her in many days. They said that sometimes she likes to do her summer work here, or just sit by the logs, looking at the pond by herself to calm down and decompress. We decided to take a chance tonight and see if she would show up. Clearly, we haven't seen her yet, so I guess we should just wait by here."

"Well, we don't mind. We enjoy spending time here—maybe you both might too," said the eldest Ledger. It was quiet for a few moments before another Ledger sibling started back up the conversation.

"Let's resume the conversation we were having earlier, and if you Shabah could give us some insight that would be very helpful. We have been thinking about how it has been living here, and what it has to offer to us, especially in this kind of town. A lot of people would rather

liked them very much for them. The Shabahs turned around to go back through the brush but were distracted by a sudden commotion.

"Oh my! What are they doing?" yelled one of the Ledger brothers in shock as all the other brothers gasped. The Shabah siblings turned around and looked behind them to see what it was that had gotten the attention of the Ledgers. In the distance, on the other side of the pond, where the jagged rocks and terrain were much more extreme, and barely visible in the darkness of the sky which had overcome the neighborhood once the sunset passed were the Lillis twins, running from a large figure who was catching up behind them.

"Who is that?" asked Cassandra, who was not yet adjusted to the darkness. Her blurry and fuzzy eyesight was making it difficult to differentiate what was moving across the pond.

"It is the Lillis twins! They are being chased by the Russian man, and his dog is right behind him—that hungry hound is keeping its pace! I wonder why they are running…" said the eldest Ledger boy. Some faint screams could be heard from the little twins who were running incredibly fast. Popov had no chance at catching those boys for they have been hiking through the grounds of the neighborhood for years, and they easily jumped and skipped through the rocks while Popov struggled to catch up. He was yelling at them to immediately stop running, but they did not. After a few more seconds of this high intensity run, the twins and Popov disappeared into the wooded area on that side of the pond, and the squeals of the boys were not heard again.

"Well, that was interesting. I wonder why they were being chased by that man," said Gabriel.

"I hope they are not injured or caught by him. I know how it feels to be chased by a crazed, murderous Russian like him, and it does not feel safe at all. Pray for those twins!" said Andra in response.

The Ledger boys immediately reeled in their homemade bait of feathers and neon colors and packed their things into a small bag. "I hope you know that those Lillis twins live relatively close to here— maybe two or three houses east—and they are definitely returning home. If you don't want to interact with the Russian again, I suggest running back home. That is why we are packing up—he does not like us that much."

The Shabah siblings did not say a word to each other and only turned to run back through the wooded area. It was much faster to get home when coming back through the woods than it was to go into them—probably because of an increase in fear—but only after a minute did they arrive back onto the road. They looked down towards the Lillis house but did not see anything. Cassandra urged them not to investigate anything at all and to only go home, and so they did, safely for the rest of the night.

Gabriel and Cassandra settled back into their kitchen, where their mother had just finished preparing some ham and potatoes for them to eat. It was still very warm, and while they ate in comfortable silence, Gabriel began to contemplate. "Why did Delilah not come to the pond today? She was the one who had managed to get information—no matter how valid—out of the Lillis twins to begin with, and yet, she never appeared. Perhaps she was busy, or perhaps she did not like me as much as I thought she would. I have never wondered so deeply about a person before," he thought.

CHAPTER XV

It was a lovely Saturday morning, a few days after the Shabah siblings went to the lake. The air was filled with the scent of the grown sunflowers by the old couple down the road, allowing the sweet smell to flow in each nose if they stepped outside, and the sun was shining with the same strength it had in the past week, cool and calm. There had not been a rainy day since last month, but there were no droughts in Quintbridge as the pond always provided a steady flow of water to whoever needed it. There was a prediction by a group of meteorologists near Delilah Candella's house who said that there will be heavy rains in a day or so—presumably tomorrow. This did upset some neighbors, who were enjoying their time basking in the fresh sunlight, but it also brought hope to some others; they had crafted their lives after agriculture, and this water would revitalize the crops nearby. Farmers had a soft spot deep in their hearts, no matter how black and ugly they had become over time or how sweet their blood was maintained, and this news of rain was sure to excite them.

Gabriel wanted to stay inside on this day, thinking it best to continue his reading of War and Peace. He adored the simplicity of Tolstoy's writing, and he was immersed in the readings. Every sentence felt like he had been propelled into the world of Russian affairs that Tolstoy created in his elaborate and detailed mind. Every word that he read was being experienced within his subconscious, where he became a fiery character watching from some omnipotent view. He spent some time distracting himself from his little affairs with Delilah and Cassandra (both his sister and his neighbor) with the characters and settings he read so profusely about. His literature was so enveloping that he could hardly hear any sound coming from downstairs; the only senses working were his sight and the occasional touch when he needed to flip a page, and his brain only generated ideas solely about his plots and their futures.

There was a quick rattle of knocks on the front door of the Shabah home, hitting the doors as if the knocker were in a hurry. Ms. Shabah opened the door confidently but was internally weary of who could be there and what they could say. Her daughter stood behind her, wanting a glimpse of what was to occur but not be involved at all. Once the door was flung open, a young teenage boy stood there, stepping in a place like he was about to pee or like he was ready to run somewhere, and he introduced himself. However, he was very quickly interrupted by the shriek of joy coming from the daughter in the background.

"Jason! Oh my, what are you doing here? I'm so happy to see you!" exclaimed Cassandra Shabah, running up to the door now so that she was not hiding in the shadows.

"Can I help you with something?" asked Ms. Shabah, looking at her child and the boy in confusion. "Yes, can we help you?" repeated Cassandra.

"Oh, not necessarily. You see, I am in a slight rush, and felt that I needed to come and tell you this news before you execute your plans for the rest of the day. I don't think I can make the piano practice today. I know that piano is usually first, and fencing second, which is why I am here to tell you that I won't be home during that time. However, I will return once it is time to begin lessons for fencing, although, it would have to be a short lesson since I will return in the time that is usually the middle of the lesson. I do need to go now, but I hope you can understand," said the boy, occasionally stumbling on and slurring his words because he was so desperate in getting them out as rapidly as possible.

"Oh, honey, that really should be no problem. Gabriel has been in his room all morning, and I don't see him coming down anytime soon. You can hurry along now. I'll send Cassandra over to you when I notice you have arrived home. Goodbye!"

"Oh, thank you! I am glad it is not troubling. Goodbye!" said Jason before sprinting back to his home, cutting through the front yard. "Goodbye, Jason! I am excited for tonight!" yelled Cassandra as he left, hoping to catch any sort of reaction from him. He never did react, though, and just continued to run, before driving away with his mother only a few seconds after he got back home.

✳   ✳   ✳

That very afternoon, at the pond, Gabriel and Andra were fishing with the Ledger boys, a habit that has developed over the past few weeks when the siblings needed some time to unwind from their whirlwind of a summer. It was late July, almost a whole two months since the beginning of the cruel new adventure that the Shabah family had been forced upon. Cassandra Farrow had still not appeared as they had hoped, leaving the children to believe that the Lillis twins were lying about the habits of the girl.

Gabriel and Andra lounged by the edge of the bond on some slimy rocks, swishing their bait around in the water to lazily attempt to allure some larger fish. They spoke very little to each other, complaining about something that happened earlier in the week, or realizing something about the neighborhood that they needed to share. Gabriel talked overwhelmingly about nature, which annoyed Andra and the Ledgers because of how boring it was to hear. There was nothing dramatic or shocking about the sun's existence in the world, prevalent in its radiation, and the trees were the same as they were before they were born and would probably stay the same for more years to come, so it was indisputably repetitive and unoriginal for him to keep talking about it.

"Gabriel, please stop talking about all of this nonsense. Who cares about the sun? The trees don't matter either. Everything is how it is, and I don't want to sit here and talk about the unchangeable," said Andra to her brother. There were groans of agreement coming from the Ledgers, who stood in silence. "Talk about something else, please. I am practically begging."

"Just because you don't understand the importance of the environment does not mean that I should stop talking about it. How about, instead of complaining, you start to focus on the content of my thoughts and their meanings?"

"How about you switch the subject from something pointless to something meaningful? I'd rather hear about your sleep at this point."

"I am going to sleep over at Delilah's tonight."

"What? Why are you doing that?" The Ledger boys tilted their heads to try and hear more clearly but tried not to make it noticeable.

"Mostly because I am sure mother will allow me to. Also, we have an arrangement in the morning: an art exhibition. Lila has been looking forward to it for weeks, and I must go with her. It is early in the morning, so I must sleep over there to get up as early as possible with her."

"Is that what you call her now? Lila?" asked Cassandra, scoffing in humor at the nickname he had given to her.

"Yes, it is."

"Is she your partner now? Your girlfriend?"

"No, although I wish she was."

"Well, I suppose if you are going to leave for the night, I am too. I am going to sleep at Jason's house then."

"No, you cannot do that. You must not do that. I won't allow it," ordered Gabriel.

"Yes, I am going to do that. You cannot forbid me from not."

"Yes, I can, and I will. You will not sleep at a boy's house this evening."

"What is the difference if you sleep at a girl's house? I am simply doing the opposite of what you are doing. Just because I am a year younger than you does not—"

"No! You are not going there," he yelled. There was a moment of silence, where the shock of his tone, back to his original pessimism that Cassandra and her mother used to experience in Fiddlefield. She was reminded of his terrible anger, where he would refuse things until there was no use in asking him for anything. However, given the circumstances, Cassandra did not listen to him, and after the event with the Russian man and the prolonged state of her ankle, she did not care about her brother's negative and dismissive thoughts.

"No, Gabriel. I am doing as I please. You are not my father and so you cannot boss me around. I abide by our mother's rules and my own, so please excuse me if I am not going to listen and apply every single piece of advice you give to me!" she said. There was a hint of anger in her voice, something that appeared occasionally, but not in this vicious way as she had just done. Gabriel stayed quiet, shocked at the words his sister said, but respectful of her decisions. It was quiet for a moment, the birds in the trees and the sound of water lapping on the rocks coming back into life, being heard again, and the children sustained it that way until the Ledger brothers started back up a conversation.

"I just noticed that Andra was talking about fathers, or that she mentioned a father," started the youngest, "and I am not sure if it is my place to ask you this, forgive me if not, but do you have a father? I noticed I have never seen an older man's presence in your home and have never heard of one either. The Farrow children don't have a father and neither does Jason from what we know. So, do you?" The Shabah looked at each other for some encouragement to speak about this subject. Gabriel gave a questioning look to Andra, seeming to ask her to confirm if he is allowed to talk about it, and she nodded her head in return, fortifying his strength to talk.

"Well, we don't have a father, but we used to. When we were back in Fiddlefield, our family was very close. It was Andra, our mother, our father, and I, always together. Our home at Fiddlefield was on a pleasant farm—hectares of land surrounding us—and it was beautiful. We did well with money, especially our mother, who secretly owned a factory business for textiles. Everything was under our father's name, but it was she who was truly exceptional at managing the factories. Anyways, our father was very adamant about farming and loved his cows and chickens as much as he loved us. He woke up at the bare beginnings of the sunrise each morning and fell asleep after he knew the rest of us were asleep and safe. He worked very hard and very well, and taught us many things about farming, like how to care for the cows and the chickens, where to look for eggs that were laid, and how to squeeze utters for milk, and we loved him for that. However, there was one component of farming and caring for the cows that our father did not like, and that was milking them. He did teach us, but he did not squeeze the utters himself; rather, he had a demonstration for us to watch. He had hired a milkmaid, and this milkmaid was the one who showed us. I think her name was Petra..." there was a pause as if he had come to a glottal stop and could not pronounce any more letters or words. He looked at Cassandra to continue the story, and she acquiesced, telling the rest of the story to the boys.

"Well anyways, Petra and our father, whose name was Frederick Shabah, were very close—they practically rose and fell together and were awake at the very same time every day. The two had a shared love of farming, beyond the normal amount of love. We believe this is what is accredited to the unknown love of the environment that Gabriel carries within him. Anyways, one day, there was a large commotion coming from the shed where the cows were housed. It was early in the morning before anyone was usually awake save our father and Petra. Petra was honestly the loveliest German woman I had ever met, and she adored our family, so this was utterly shocking. But supposedly, our mother had walked into the shed to let our father know that he had left the fire on in our house overnight, which could have burned the house completely if some stray coal would have hit some flammable material. When she walked into the shed, she stopped and peered from the side of a wall, where she saw Petra seducing our father. Our mother told us that 'Frederick was seduced by that German girl,' but we do not believe that. He always awoke much earlier than we did, and stayed awake much later, and so did Petra. When we heard that she was forcing him to feel her breasts and to touch her around the private areas, we knew deep down that it was not forced. It was an affair that must have been around for a while. The nerve that Petra had to teach us to milk a cow while hiding the fact that she was with our father secretly the entire time is beyond me. After witnessing what she witnessed, our mother came back to us, told us everything, and planned for us to leave the city for someplace else. She saw that a space was available here, and for the next couple of weeks, we shunned our father. The town heard of the adultery, and Petra was soon gone, probably back to Germany. We left immediately and moved here, and since, it has been wonderful. We don't think about our father much—he has become more of a blurry vision, something that isn't real, than an actual person who raised us. He spent so much time in the shed or the fields, either with the milkmaid or tending to our pastures. I'd say the only good thing to ever come out of those fields was the butter—the milkmaid was incredible at churning. However, we don't miss Petra or Frederick at all. Not at all."

The boys were stunned at the anecdote of their father and seemed empathic to their experience, offering solace to them. "Well, we are so sorry. That sounds like a terrible fate—an awful end to your father's involvement in your lives. If you need anything at all, please, let us know."

"We are very well off now; there is no need to comfort us. This happened a few weeks before we moved here, and the event was so disgraceful that we couldn't even bare to miss him or wish he hadn't done anything as he had. It was such an embarrassment—such a shame," said Cassandra. Once again, this awkward silence that plagued this interaction between the boys and the siblings was present. "Does anyone know the time?" asked Cassandra, attempting to break this unpleasantness.

"Yes, I have a pocket watch with me. Let's see. It is about a quarter to five." said the eldest Ledger boy. Once he mentioned his pocket watch, the rest of his brothers groaned in covetousness, thinking that they were worthy of the pocket watch more than their eldest brother.

"Oh, God! Gabriel, we must leave, it is getting too late. If we don't ask mother now, she won't let us go. She doesn't want you or me going out during the nighttime, especially with what happened with Popov. Gabriel, get up! We have to go!" urged Andra, pushing Gabriel while he was balancing on some large rock and watching him fall into a small puddle mixed with mud and dry soil. He quickly got up, brushed off the muck and dirt on his shirt and shorts from his lazy nap on the rock, and said goodbye to the Ledger brothers with his sister. Cassandra already knew her plan of how to go out with Jason that night, but Gabriel was nervous about what he needed to say. Cassandra was also fearful about what Gabriel was going to say, for her plan relied on the success of her brother. While they crossed the road and walked back home, through the cool shadows of the trees and the wind flowing through their hair, they practiced what to say and how to say it, hoping only for the optimal outcome.

CHAPTER XVI

Ms. Shabah was cooking something warm and sloppy in the kitchen, and once the children could smell what food was being prepared, they gagged. It was a putrid smell, like something rotten had infested the house and spread itself on the walls and the floors, like it, could not be avoided. Gabriel and Cassandra looked at each other in disgust and walked into the kitchen to see their mother, desperate in trying to ignore the revolting smell.

"Hello, mother," said the children.

"Well, hello my darlings! You both arrived right before I finish dinner. It is a kind of stew—sloppy and brown. But it has the most divine smell!" said Ms. Shabah, clearly proud of her cooking.

"Yes—we *absolutely* agree. We have a couple of questions if you don't mind us asking," said Gabriel.

"Sure. What is it?"

"Well, I was wondering if I could sleep at Delilah's house tonight. There is an art exhibition that she invited me to, and it is early tomorrow morning—"

"Certainly not, Gabriel! You will not be sleeping with a girl, especially if you have only known her for the time you have known her for."

"But mother, you didn't even hear my reasoning!"

"I won't allow it."

"Mother! Listen to me! I am not sleeping with her because I am in love with her; it is for a completely different reason. Tomorrow is the art exhibition she has been talking about forever. We have planned it for weeks, and it is very early in the morning. The time window is from six to ten, which is only four early hours in the morning. She needs to go to see all the art for some passion project she is doing, and I promised her that I would come with her. I am going over because I have had a lot of trouble waking up in the mornings, and I don't want her to be upset with me because of my failure to get out of bed. If I sleep there, she will be sure to wake me up, and I can actually go to her exhibition," he said while puffing. It seemed to take a lot of energy to say the words he wished she would accept.

"I can wake you up, Gabriel. You do not need to sleep with a girl, especially with your age."

"Mother, I hope you aren't thinking I am going to do anything remotely gross. I am not that kind of child, and I wouldn't even do that as an adult. I have morals and I intend to enforce them for the good of the world and myself." Ms. Shabah turned around to face him, dropping her spoon into the slop. She ignored it, though, and maintained her eye contact.

"Well—I suppose you may go. If you are to leave with her for the night, I expect that you make sure to remain classy. The last thing I need in this world is some letter from that woman across the road explaining how my children are 'ruining the purity of the neighborhood' so please stay smart."

"I will, mother. Do not worry," he said. He seemed extremely relieved at her acceptance of his idea; he knew that she would be difficult to convince, but this confirmed her leniency for Cassandra. She looked at her brother with a smirk and then began her paragraph of complimentary remarks.

"Mother, this sloppy stew looks and smells delightful, and I cannot wait to try it. Also, where did you get this summer dress? It is beyond gorgeous, and I want some clothing similar to that. Your style is unmatched, and I wish that I had the same taste in fashion as you do. Anyways, I wanted to ask the same question for you as Gabriel did, except that instead of Delilah, I wanted to go with Jason. There is a short film tonight in town—the Cinderella short—and it looks lovely! I thought it would be a great idea to go watch it with him after our lesson. He is such a fine boy; don't you think so?"

"Cassandra Shabah, absolutely not. Not a day on Earth will I allow you to sleep with a boy under my household! This is not negotiable," said Ms. Shabah.

"Mother! How unfair you are! You let Gabriel go with Delilah, which could have a scenario far more egregious than mine. I am literally next door, and Gabriel is on the opposite side of this massive neighborhood. I am also far more responsible than Gabriel is, and you cannot let him go without also letting me go! Aren't I also supposed to be in pursuit of a husband soon? Jason is a perfect choice, and I know that you believe it too."

"Well, then. It seems both of my children will be going out tonight," said Ms. Shabah. The girl smiled brightly, showing off her white teeth and perfectly shaped lips. Gabriel also smirked, excited that his original plans are coming to life. He wished he could preserve this moment forever—where he got everything and anything he asked for—and felt as if every piece of a puzzle were finally coming together to make sense. "You must stay responsible, though. I don't want you doing anything naughty, and to remain calm. Also, you are both liars. I know this stew is horrid, and the smell is so awful that I think I might be sick. Don't lie to me to try and get your way. Lying only provides a temporarily short path: a path filled with spikes and traps, and so it is always worth it to be honest when you can have a safer path. It may be longer, but it won't get you into trouble. Don't ever risk lying to get your way with me again. Go fetch something to eat from the market, please, and get something for me to eat as well."

The children felt embarrassed. They didn't know why they continued attempting to persuade their mother by lying, trying to trick her, deceive her, because it never worked. Ms. Shabah knew her children inside-out, every groove and bump on their bodies that could have ever been forged was known by the woman, and it caused a lot of embarrassment when they continuously attempted to fool her. The children quickly agreed to get food and went to the market and bought some eggs and tomatoes to make a lovely omelet. Ms. Shabah was going to throw the food out into the yard for the bacteria to eat but decided that she might offer it to the Victoriana couple; it was still edible, and they wouldn't have to live off the dumpster food that they had eaten all this time. When she offered it, they accepted it with gratitude and ate it happily. They specifically commented on the warmth of the food, stating how they haven't had a warm meal in quite some time—it was difficult adjusting to their new lifestyle. They were grateful, and hid back under their home, underneath the same rags. It was relatively warm outside, but that did not stop them from covering up; they were so terrified of the women upstairs finding them and expelling them from the neighborhood.

Ms. Shabah suddenly recognized that she had a wonderful love for helping the people around her. There was something satisfying about giving the warm slop to the Victorianas, even if it was not as tasty as she wished it to be, and there was also something fulfilling in allowing her children a night of fun even if the worries she had of their safety and their actions tormented her for hours. She had a pure soul underneath all her hypocrisy, brimming with hopes that there would be no drama to subconsciously spread, or that there would be anything harming the best people. She hoped that the malicious were damned, and the world would remain loyal and faithful to itself. Yet, they were only hopes. They disappeared in mere seconds, her thoughts of the future burning as lived through her reality.

Once she sat back down, she was gifted with her omelet, which she enjoyed in both tastes and smells much more than her brown slop. Her children sat with her, eating the omelets that they had prepared as well, and then departed into the night for their sleepovers. They were excited about what the night beheld, each just as curious as the other.

Once they went outside, the siblings gave each other one final look for the night, smiling widely and anxiously. Cassandra turned to the right, taking the same path that Jason Grealm had done earlier when he left in such a hurry, while Gabriel turned to the left, going along the everlasting path toward Delilah Candella's house.

CHAPTER XVII

Upon the last step to the front door of the Grealm household, Jason opened the door and looked at Cassandra with a sly grin. He had been watching her from the moment she stepped foot onto his estate and saw that she had been skipping along the grass and the stones like a small child who had realized it was Christmas day. It startled Cassandra, but she did not mind once she saw who was standing at the door, awaiting her arrival.

"Hello, dearest Andra. I was not sure that you would come here tonight, considering that I returned three hours ago. I was just sitting here, reading a book when I felt the most peculiar urge to look outside for something, and that is when I saw your beautiful dress flowing in the night breeze coming right towards me," said Jason.

"Well, I figured that I better get here as quick as possible because I was outside all day and had forgotten all about time and its slow-but-paced movement. I went inside and saw my mother cooking the most awful stew I have ever seen, so Gabriel and I went to the market to get some new ingredients to make some omelets for dinner. I doubt she even saw you come home at all, but nevertheless, I am here! Also, there are a couple more things I want to mention. There will be a showing of the short new film Cinderella, and—this is the biggest news of all, and I am praying that your mother allows it—I can sleep over tonight!" cheered Cassandra. Jason's mouth gaped open like he was in surprise, but then laughed in happiness—he had always had a plan for Cassandra to sleep over in case they were ever allowed to.

"Well, isn't it our lucky night? Do you want to begin the lesson now?" asked Jason.

"Jason, dear, never mind about the lesson! We can do so many other things now. We have the freedom of the entire night and morning to do whatever we please, whether that be eating ice cream and chocolates or if that is staying up all night long."

"Well, I suppose so. When shall we go see the film?"

"Now, if you can."

"Oh, that is good. I need to get out of the house. Mother is so terribly distracted with somebody here that she won't even notice me gone. I'll get the bicycles."

"Who is at your house? Am I intruding?"

"I am not sure who it is, but no, you are never intruding here." He prepared some bicycles for them, and they quickly raced to the showing of Cinderella. The atmosphere was magical that night, racing seductively down the roads of Quintbridge to see who can get to the showing fastest and laughing as one took over the other. They were neck-in-neck but ultimately, Jason took the final advantage and arrived at the showing of Cinderella before she did.

They were close to the church, the lovely cathedral erected proudly over the rest of the town, and the stained glass casting its images in vibrant colored light across the grounds, but the showing was next to the church. A silver screen was placed on a large wooden wall and small hints of light were gently pressed against its surface, and it overlooked a small patch of a field where some people were sitting, waiting for the silver screen to project the motion picture. The screen would brighten and darken with the movement of the light, showing an array of images or symbols that no one had seen before. It was currently stuck on the number thirteen, where the countdown was beginning for the movie but was inexplicably stuck on this number. Nobody thought anything about it, save for the fact that the crowd of viewers was beginning to get annoyed by the discontinuation of the countdown.

Engineers hurried to restart the countdown, and after a couple of minutes, the numbers began to move again, down to one, until the motion picture began its course. There, in the sweet twilight of the town of Quintbridge, Cinderella pleaded with her stepsisters to allow her to go to the ball. The fascinating movement of the women on the screen, moving only by the light that the projector created, made the eyes of Jason and Andra wonder. They held each other as the background transformed and the dances and cheers began. Witchcraft transformed objects into people, like the rats into men, and this transformation created an exciting fear inside Andra, where she held onto Jason tighter. Once Cinderella had transformed, the crowd released marvelous applause, congratulating the directors and actors on their incredibly exquisite performance. However, in the corner, a small child waved a magnifying glass that he had gotten from his father's glasses.

The light refracted into a focused beam on the silver screen, and some small smoke emerged. Only after a short while did the beam transform into another mode of light, that of the petrifying orange, and it ate through the screen at an alarming rate. Screams of horror emerged from the crowd as they saw the film being eaten away by the light, and the seated crowd shot up from their seats and ran away. "The church! Save the church!" yelled people from each corner of the town. The flame had begun to reach larger heights than anyone could have imagined, and it was grazing the sides and edges of the church, scaring the mass of people who went to this church each Sunday, and particularly creating fear in those who planned to attend the mass tomorrow. The flame dissipated, though, and all that was left was a black and grey screen with small hints of the lovely Cinderella motion picture continuing to play. The ballerina was beginning her pirouettes when the crowd completely vanished. Jason and Andra had left too and were biking home.

"That was horrid! How did that even happen? I cannot believe we witnessed that—survived that, even—and now we are biking home!"

"I know, Andra. That was truly incredible, and not in a good way. How did that happen—I will never know. Now that it is gone, though, I guess the only thing we have left to do is relax at home and read or something. I have gathered some paints in case we wanted to do something more than just read."

"Well, that sounds lovely. Maybe I will paint the failure of the Cinderella showing that just occurred! Ha!" said she.

"Don't make jokes, Andra, that makes you seem heartless. It wasn't too bad. At least we got to see the beginning parts of it. Shame that it all went down in flames, though. I hope the church is all right since I will not bear having that lost. If that beautiful building, is coated with the fine drawings of Jesus and Mother Mary, and how beautiful they are, I will be devastated. Oh, God—Andra…"

"Oh, God! Jason! You know what that means if it is burnt to a crisp! We will be cursed, and not by some witch or wizard, but by the Devil himself! A religious curse! I can bet confidently that a religious curse is far more detrimental than a regular curse by some evil spell. This curse will come from the beings in the sky—the ones who made us from the scraps of clay on the ground and give life to everything around us. And I disagree with you about the Cinderella showing being 'not too bad.' It was awfully bad. It could have been better if there was more to it, and it wasn't burnt down," she said with a cruel tone. Andra had changed from her original feelings of appreciation and wonder to a sudden hatred of the circumstances that had just occurred.

"I don't believe so. I have an appreciation for the film we saw, and I suggest you find one too. It was still mesmerizing to watch, and we cannot just disregard that. However, if that church did burn, we are going to the pits of hell. Andra, if it burned down, it was definitely because of us. I just feel it. I don't know why, but I feel that if it burned down, it is probably our fault in some way or another."

"Jason, we didn't even do anything."

"I know. I just have an eerie feeling."

"If anything, it is the fault of an unintelligent engineer or whoever created the fire in the first place."

"Well, yes, if we look at it from a literal perspective. But I have this terrifying feeling that us being there tonight created this fire in the first place. It is so rare for something to uncontrollably burn like that and has no one in the entire sitting area to see. So incredibly rare, Andra!"

"Perhaps you are just guilty that it burnt down. I really don't see how this has anything to do with us. We merely sat and watched the film with no intention to create dramatic problems like that. I think, when we get back, we should just relax or something."

"Well, alright. Maybe I am just overthinking. Compensating for some catastrophe."

"Exactly. I think we should go back and just paint or something. Something that could bring us back to the calm reality we are in instead of thinking about that fire."

The two children walked back inside quietly. Jason didn't want to draw attention to his mother. He thought it would be important to keep quiet because he still heard that unfamiliar voice in the wine cellar—a gruff, manly voice—laughing and talking along with the mellow pitch of his mother. When there were guests in the Grealm household, he was never to disturb them—if he did, his mother would get extremely angry at the poor boy, and would curse him terribly until he felt the sickening feeling she would describe as 'what she felt when she was disrupted by the boy'—and so he simply went back up to his room, where he would try to drown out any curious noise he would here with a book or by attempting to sleep it out. He asked Andra to follow him up the stairs to his room, away from any noise of the man and his mother. Once they walked inside, he pulled two canvases from inside a closet, as well as some linseed oil, oil paints, cloths, a few paintbrushes of different sizes, and some turpentine to wash the paint out of the brushes thoroughly. He sat everything down on his floor and brought a magnificent quilt to put over the two as they painted. It felt like soft cotton and had dyes of every color of the rainbow on there, which weaved artistic and vivid details of different flowers and landscapes.

Andra decided to paint exactly what she had intended to: an expression of the fire. She drew in the colors of orange, red, white, and black, but then conserved the blue to use to draw God above, angry and malevolent, observing everything occurring, but with his eyes focusing on the couple. This picture she drew was an image that was created in her head by the words of Jason—the boy she began to like, with his blond hair and his clear skin always cleansing her mind of negative thoughts and bringing pastels into her vision—and the fear she had for this curse that Jason was so sure of was portrayed deeply. She felt uneasy painting it, but attempted to find some humor, as that seemed to always fix her feelings in the right manner. She purposefully painted the head of God as much larger, seeming foolish and silly, and made the fire into the shape of a divorced couple—making herself laugh. This drawing only took her a couple of hours, the same time it took Jason to make his painting.

While she began to paint, Jason pondered for some moments until he thought of what he wanted to paint. He wanted to distract himself from the event that had happened, and thus chose something to draw that was relatively unrelated. He started to paint the engorged and large body of an owl, using as many colors as he could muster, and created a beautiful portrait of a rainbow owl, staring intently at the viewer. It seemed to be confrontational, asking the viewers themselves what they see and what it means. Its eyes were large and circular, more than usual, and its small pupils were deeply frightening. Jason was slightly afraid of what he had drawn and decided to try to fix it. He made the owl's eyes smaller, almost shut, with only a sliver of green shimmering among the vibrance of color. Next to the owl, he decided to paint a small raven, looking at the owl itself. It was black and dull, not even detailed, as it was just a small smudge in the figure of a bird. Once he finished, he turned to Andra to see if she had finished her painting and saw that she was mostly done. They turned to each other, hiding their art from each other, and began to count down from three, ready to turn the paintings to each other for the other to see. Once it was time, they both eagerly presented their work.

Jason dropped his painting and looked at what Cassandra had painted in irritation.

"Did you draw that on purpose? To taunt me, or ridicule me or something?" he asked, shaking his head as he spoke. He was clearly angry with her for not taking him seriously before.

"No? I did not. Why? What is wrong with it? I told you I was going to paint what happened, and so I painted everything that happened as you said it," she said in defense. She seemed confused by his sudden change of emotions.

"Andra, look at what you painted. God's head, which I am assuming is God, is so large that it looks ridiculous. You painted the fire to be some people arguing or something, and it looks like you don't even care about what happened. People could have died, and you made a joke out of it! Why are acting like this whole thing was nothing? God is going to come after us for this, especially you for painting him like he is some inflated idiot."

"Jason! How dare you! Why are you being so sensitive? I simply painted a picture. It seemed too dark so I changed it a little bit, so I don't have to look at some depressing image. I wanted this to be fun, and it turned a little sour because of you. Stop yelling at me like this."

"I am not yelling; I am only saying that what you painted could be a bad omen. I feel like this whole night is just foreshadowing something terrible to happen, especially with us, and I can't help but fear it. Don't tell me that you don't feel any shame for what happened."

"Jason, this is the last I am going to speak of this because it is beginning to make me angry. There was a fire. There was a *fire*. Nothing else. A fire may have burnt the church down, and if it did, it did. There is nothing we could have done to cause such a catastrophe like this. I appreciate you coming with me to watch the film, which admittedly didn't turn out to be much, but you cannot sit here and yell at me that it was a bad omen when nothing happened at all. We have nothing to worry about because we didn't do anything. Stop acting like a little child Jason! My God!" she said. She was flustered by his intoxicating fear and how easily this fear controlled him. She believed he should not have been shouting at her as he had been, and so she decided to shut him up about this subject for the rest of the time.

There was a long moment of silence in the room, where Jason and Andra could hear the breathing and blinking of the other, and muffled booms of laughter from downstairs nervously floated through the walls. Andra, still reveling in her anger, turned around aggressively to face the door, striving to hear anything of what was going on downstairs, before turning back to face Jason once again. His face seemed petrified, but he played it off skillfully as being confused by her strange behavior.

"Jason, what are you hiding from me?"

"Nothing. Why are you asking me that?"

"You have been acting weird all night, and I cannot help but think that I know you know who is downstairs. Is that the reason why you have been acting weird? What are you hiding?"

"I don't know anything!" he defensively claimed. "I am not hiding anything from you, I promise that."

"You were in the house before I was even here, and that same voice was there too. You definitely know who it is, and if you don't tell me, I am going to go down there myself and look at who it is," yelled Andra, becoming increasingly frustrated at his lack of humility and raising her voice with every inch of sentence that she formed.

"We will go down together, then. I do not know anything." Jason was very impressed with her thoughts. He was indeed hiding something from her but did not want to communicate it so that she feels comfortable. Her identification of his secret was unexpected to him, but he continued to be oblivious to her assertions.

"Get up, then. We shall see," she said forcefully. Cassandra was keen on knowing who was there, for she knew that Jason was keeping his knowledge of the man hidden. There wasn't anyone she expected to be down there, so she was equally as curious as to who it could be. Jason held her by the arm, and they descended the staircase as quietly as possible. Jason knew that they were drunk so their sensitivity to noise would be reduced, and with each creak, he assured Andra that there was nothing to be afraid of. Once they were at the point of the stairs where they could bend down to peer at who was talking through the glass in the wine cellar, they did. Andra went first.

Down she went, slowly bending her knees to see what was inside that glass cellar she always sees. On the emerald sofa, underneath the warmth of a dark green silk blanket, was Jason's mother, her slips smeared with the red lipstick that she always wears, and next to her was a man, his arm wrapped around her neck and resting on her shoulder. She laid her head on his shoulder, laughing while they sipped their wine. The light was not yet brightening the face of the man, so she could not see who it is, but she did not move from her crouch. Jason crouched down next to her, and peered just as intently, waiting for the man to move his head in the face of the light. He slowly rose his head, appearing to have his lips stained with the same lipstick as the woman. It seemed to move in slow motion, up and closer to the light, revealing more of his slender, tanned face, until, in a single movement, he looked directly at the light, revealing his eyes and forehead. Cassandra clasped her agape mouth with the palm of her hand once she realized who the man that was cuddling with Jason's mother was: the Russian man.

Just as Cassandra and Jason were about to rush back upstairs to their room, she noticed that Bonnie and the Russian man laughed again, before looking at each other and kissing softly on the lips. Cassandra let out a small grunt of surprise, quiet enough for the two on the sofa to not hear but for Jason to know that she was angry. She stood back up and walked to Jason's room, spewing frustration and confusion from her breaths with each step she took up the flight of stairs and into the hallway. Once she entered, she stood with her back facing the door and waited for the sound of Jason's feet to tap their way into the bedroom and close the door softly to not disturb the couple downstairs.

Immediately, she turned around, her dress rising with the spin like the tutu of a ballerina, and, in one swift and clean motion, she extended her arm and hand out and slapped him across the face, the clap of thunder coming from the impact. He emitted a small grunt of pain, reaching for his hand with his trembling fingers; he was unable to reach them, though, and with the back of her hand, like she was facing a difficult and speedy tennis rally, Andra hit his other side of the face with the back of her palm. Two red marks, detailing the outlines of her delicate fingers, stained the cheeks of the boy. "You liar! You filthy, disgusting, rat-faced liar! I will never trust you again! The way you disrespected me tonight by keeping the secret of your mother's affair with the man who tried to get me arrested—arrested for *murder*! You kept quiet, and for that, you deserved those two pain-stricken slaps."

"Andra, I am so sorry. Please, calm down. I must explain this to you."

"What is there to explain? I saw exactly what is happening with my own eyes, and you betrayed me for not saying anything to me. You are the filth underneath my shoes, and the way I will make sure to stomp even harder when I walk out of this house will be loud enough for you to hurt. Hurt as I hurt. How sad I am!" she screamed. There was a deafening silence in the room without her talking, and the tears that filled her eyes were slowly dribbling out onto her smooth and clean face. The swelling and tender redness on the outside corners of her eyes made Jason feel guilty for lying about not having any knowledge of the events downstairs, and his tear ducts began to precipitate the same droplets as hers.

They stood there, crying together, Jason attempting to feel the very same pain as his companion in the room. They were not yet official to each other as partners and soulmates but felt like they did not need to say it verbally. It emotionally pained Cassandra to slap Jason across the face, and although she desperately wanted to leave the house and never speak to the boy again, she could only stand in place, paralyzed by her feelings of betrayal and disloyalty. Bad faith was ripping through the thin threads of silk that made their relationship binding, and all that they could do was cry and hope it would be better. Once they had reached a level where they were able to communicate without weeping dramatically as they had before, the two began to speak.

"Andra, I want us to not think of what is going on downstairs. I do not like to think about it, and for me, it is better to just waste my time doing other pointless things than emotionalize over what is happening. My mother is her own person, and there is only one reason why I did not want to tell you any of this. It is because I care about you. Every lesson we have in fencing, every interaction we have had since living here, has led me to care about you more than myself. It was when I was able to guide you on the board that the Ledgers created that I finally felt myself carefully contemplating which words I should say and which I should not. To think how I think is to die in an angel's arms. I must tell you this now because I don't know when else I could ever." The two stood there, in the same positions as they had stayed before, and he continued. "I love you, Cassandra Shabah. We have only known each other for a few weeks, and I am already so in love that I cannot bear being around the prickliness of being alone when I am not with you. I love you until I am only a withering soul among the abundance of energy in the world, where I am incapable of love. But until that time comes, I will love you forever, Cassandra."

She felt that she had finally heard what she had wanted to hear forever. The two were inseparable, and although she wanted to leave so desperately, she could not. In fact, she did not say anything except move to his bed staring at him. He took that as a motive to move into the bed with her, and underneath the sheets, they held each other, radiating a frustrating love. They did not think about the future or what was going on downstairs and only fell asleep. Their own emotions had drained them of any energy they had left, sucking them into deep fatigue, where, once they lay down in the comfortable bed, they fell asleep immediately.

104

It was in the morning when the room brightened much lighter than it had before that Andra considered what she saw once again.

It smelled like grapes downstairs, probably from the absurd amounts of wine that had been drunk, and from the exhales of the couple who had now passed out on the couch that filled the air, and Cassandra prepared for her to leave. She knew Jason was still comfortably asleep in his bed, but before she left, Cassandra whispered to him.

"I am going to go now. Should I say anything to my mother about downstairs? And, also, us?" she mumbled. His eyes were still closed, and he wet his mouth with his saliva before speaking again.

"No, don't," was all he said. He groaned again, and moved his head toward the pillow, pulling the cotton sheets back up to cover his face.

"Alright, I won't." He looked peaceful and rested while he stayed in slumber. She gave him a smile that he did not see and then moved off the bed to go back toward her home. She was certainly telling her mother what she experienced.

CHAPTER XVIII

The winding roads of Quintbridge, ever-so-smooth in their complexion and lined with the most fantastic flowers anyone within the state could have ever seen, were hypnotizing Gabriel as he walked down. The slight breeze made him sliver through each letterbox and flower bush like a sly cat, brisking around the night for minutes at a time before considering his actual destination. There was something about nature and the environments that drew him close like he had some actual affection for the plants and the green growth that made everything that it is. It was not just the environment that had caused a deep sense of love and longing for his existence and the world's existence, but what was above, in the sea of black covered in sparkling dots of white, nuanced his tenderness to the Earth. The big, grey, yellow moon called to him, forcing his gaze upon the celestial creature to be frozen and wanderlust.

Everything around Gabriel distracted him as he made his way to Delilah's home. It was the fault of nature that made him do everything he was doing, like picking at the flowers and watching a moth blindly fly around, looking for a stable platform to rest upon during the night, and noticing the black pupils that made themselves see among such a rarity of light. Gabriel was infatuated with nature, not like anything else he had ever seen, and yet, the one thing that surpassed nature was the paramount love for Delilah that he felt.

Once he saw the red-accented, bruised home that sheltered the lovely girl, he gracefully walked up and knocked softly on the door. There, in a confused daze, stood Delilah, wearing only a silk pajama, and she kindly asked what he was doing in the twilight of the night at her front door.

"I am here to see you. I know that the art exhibition is tomorrow, and you must know that I am a terrible sleeper. There is nothing worse than planning something in the future just to sleep through it by the fault of your laziness. Once, I slept through an entire day of school, all the way until two o'clock, just because I refused to allow myself to get out of bed. And so, by my own intellect, I decided that I am going to come over here and possibly sleep here so that in the morning, you can help me wake up so we can look at some of this special art. I would never want to miss any sort of event like this, especially one with you, my sweet. Is that alright with you?"

"Oh, well, yes. But you must be very quiet, dear Gabriel. I cannot allow you to get me in trouble, especially with a boy in my room, on the night before my exhibition. I have been looking forward to this for weeks, and this cannot be ruined by your selfish impulses," she said with a sneaky smile. There was a large amount of chemistry playing in this interaction, drawing two poles of opposite attraction closer to each other by the mode of sarcasm and affectionate affirmations and anecdotes. Oh, how he loved her, and how she loved him!

Gabriel noticed that there was the same layout for bedsheets and pillows as before when he slept on the ground at her house during his episode of hysteria. He sat down on his pillows, the same ones with Spanish print and enhanced with deep colors of red and purple. He enjoyed watching his Lila walk around the room silently, picking through her trays of books and records, and looking for something that she could not find in the messy array of her room. She picked up a small bottle of liquid, presumably water, and tapped it with the tips of her finger. She then put some of the water on her face, leaving her skin gleaming and shiny afterward, and leaving Gabriel in wonder. In an almost whisper, she began to speak.

"This is how I wash my face. Just like bathing yourself at nighttime or in the morning, I like to wash my face with this cup of water. It feels refreshing, and the cold feeling, or wet feeling—I cannot tell—feels incredible at this time and temperature. We need to sleep, though. We have a big morning tomorrow, and if we do not sleep right now, we won't have enough time to get through every exhibit because we will be so exhausted. I will make sure to get you up extra early so the fatigue can wear off before the event. Goodnight, Gabriel!"

"Goodnight, Lila." He did not speak any further than that, and he laid his head on the pillows before drifting to sleep. Her room smelled like roses, and the sheets and pillows that she accommodated for him were as soft as ever. He felt like he was winning in his time at Quintbridge, even though it had only been for a few months, and knew that this neighborhood had begun to treat him. He reflected on his pessimisms from the past and knew that they used to harm people, but then recognized that they had all disappeared once he met Delilah. Will he ever find power in a woman so strong as to completely alter his emotional senses?

In the morning, he was shaken awake by Delilah and realized he had no dream. It was only a blink, and he did not remember falling out of consciousness, but just knew that it had happened, probably from a routine of all these years. When he was angry, he had many dreams, but now he slept as peacefully and unbothered as any lamb in the fields or baby pig after drinking its mother's breast milk. He got ready with the same clothes he was wearing yesterday—they were suitable enough for the event—and saw Delilah in a dress of only white. Her skin was golden and olive with this dress, and the light reflected onto her smile, giving her teeth a whiter shine than ever before. He noticed her beauty. She had an everlasting, classic beauty.

They left out the door and walked to the farmer's market. There was a smoky tang in the air, which they thought was a little odd, but Delilah insisted it was probably the fault of some crazy exhibition they were going to see that involved smoke or fire. It was not unusual, because it was art, but they felt like they entered a bizarre of marvelous cultural arts. There were caravans with canvases of bright colors and dull colors leaning against them; women were standing by some large, important piece of art, and explaining the history and meanings, as well as various interpretations of their works; strings were extending across the hallways of art that they walked through, covering the sky and casting an ominous shade onto the halls of art. It all seemed like fantasy to Gabriel.

People walked in and out of hallways made of the canvases and colors of the Spanish heritage, drawing crowds at some artwork that clearly spoke of controversy, and keeping some lingering people at other less intriguing works. Gabriel and Delilah stopped at each work, astonished at each specific detail. Nothing went unnoticed when Delilah was there, as she explained each detail of every piece and its special significance—it underscored her intelligence—and although Gabriel thought it was rather boring, he allowed her to speak and replenish with excitement. This exhibition, although mundane to Gabriel, lasted a few hours before they made their way back to the neighborhood.

Delilah was the only one talking. Gabriel never had a chance to speak about any of the artwork, but he did not want to, he only wanted to listen to what she wanted to say. He thought the artwork was overrated and bad but thought her ideas were intelligent and sophisticated. There was a tang to her voice when she spoke of the art, that made her seem like a raging fire of passion. Each piece was spoken about as if it were a precious child that she cared for, adopted, or even birthed herself, like an extension of her soul. He waited until she safely walked inside her home, and then went back to his own house. It was such a coincidence to see that his sister was also walking inside the house at the same time he was like she had been out of the neighborhood at the exact same time he did.

She looked at him with soft eyes, inviting him to stand with her and walk into the house together. He did so without even saying anything: this was a power that these siblings had—an unspoken action that they just knew of. She seemed distressed and concerned as if there was some prickle on the tip of her tongue that she needed to desperately spit out. She walked with jitters and shakes, and she looked like she was going to collapse from something in her mind.

CHAPTER XIX

"Mother! Mother! Where are you?" called Cassandra Shabah as she walked into the front door with her brother.

"Why are you yelling like that, Andra? We just got here—don't raise your voice," demanded Gabriel. He looked down at her behavior and assumed that she would turn to him to apologize or argue, but, instead, she ran forward, screaming for her mother. Gabriel followed her intently, curious to see what urgent news she was to present. They went outside to the plant garden, where Ms. Shabah was tending to some flowers that she started to grow.

"Mother! Mother!" she continued.

"What? Why are you screaming my name?" said Ms. Shabah, quite perplexed at her daughter's behavior.

"Oh, good mother, you need to sit down. I must tell you what occurred last night."

"Cassandra, I am not in the mood for your gossip. Can't you see that I am busy with flowers? If you want to gossip so badly, you can bore Gabriel. You know how much I despise gossip, don't you?"

"Mother, sit—now," she demanded. The tone in her voice was serious. Gabriel and Ms. Shabah knew that something of the insane nature of Quintbridge had occurred once again, and they composed themselves to a state of meditation, trying to swallow their inevitable rage down as far as they could, and sat down on the couches outside. There was a slight chirp of the birds in the trees underneath a grey sky, and the leaves chattered with the movement of the wind, serenely calming the family until Cassandra began her recapitulation of yesternight.

"It began when I walked downstairs, and the distinct smell of cigars and grapes slapped me in the face," began the girl. "I could barely hear a voice, deep and low, coming from the couches where the wine cellars are. I tried to ask Jason who it was, but he refused to tell me, which made me believe that he might have been hiding something from me. I tried peering from behind the staircase to see who was talking but couldn't see anything at all; my vision was obstructed by the enormous amounts of furniture. It was something that would distract me all night: who was it talking with Jason's mother? Anyways, we continued the night, we saw Cinderella on the big screen, but it burned down, which everyone thought was a bad omen except me. Jason especially thought it was a sign of terrible luck; a misfortune that will occur very soon. As a normal human being would do, I asked him why he was so stressed about this event happening, and all he could say was that there was nothing to be stressed about but to only know that there is a bad omen occurring. We went back upstairs to his room, and we started to paint pictures."

Ms. Shabah sighed once she heard that. "Will you just get on with it, girl? I don't care about the paintings or anything else that your children do. I need to get back to my gardening."

"I will mother, but it is necessary! So, we continued with the paintings, and I thought it would be a good idea to paint the scene of the Cinderella movie burning to flames, but then I thought it was too serious, so I added in some small details like the fire as a divorcing couple in the middle of an argument, and some other details that I thought were funny. Then, once we both finished our paintings, we showed each other, and he thought I was mocking him by drawing small, humorous images throughout the painting of the Cinderella film. I told him that he wouldn't be so sensitive about all of this if he just told me what he was hiding, and of course, the idiot claimed he was hiding nothing at all. I know that he knew who was downstairs because he was inside the house before I was even there, so I plainly asked him, 'who is downstairs?' He, once again, said that there was no one down there worth looking at and that he did not know, so I left the room myself. Being the type of person that does not take anyone's answers as the truth until I witness it for myself, I walked down the stairs, loud and proud, until I came across who had been downstairs all along, and it was nobody other than the evilest man to have ever step foot upon this grand Earth. It was the revolting Popov, the Russian man that tried to get me in trouble with the police, but there was literally no evidence against me in the first place."

Ms. Shabah shrieked in shock. He sat completely straight and clasped her mouth with both of her palms. "Please tell me this is a joke, Cassandra. Please, I am begging you," she whimpered.

"It is not a joke, mother. He was with sitting with Bonnie Grealm and laughing with her before he caught notice of me. I was standing there, obviously shocked, but did not show it, and maintained full angry composure. He looked at me with those hungry eyes of his, like he was trying to get me in trouble again, and then stuffed his tongue down Bonnie's throat like he was about to devour her. She seemed to enjoy it too, because after he let go of her, she sat on top of him and smiled, before willingly kissing him again. It was too much to bear, so I just went to sleep, but then I remembered that Jason was to sleep in the same room as me, leaving me in a panic. I calmly asked to be moved to another room, and instead of insisting that I sleep in the same room as him, he allowed me to. Just like that. He then asked me to keep my mouth shut about this or I will face the consequences of his mother and the Russian, which I thought was extremely strange. In the morning, which is now, I rushed over here to tell you about everything that has happened, and now, I am sorry, mother. Please know that I tried acting as strong as I could in that situation, but I am truly sorry for that. Who knew that she was such a backstabber?"

Ms. Shabah was at a loss for words and after a few moments of silence, where she simply stared in front of herself with nothing being spoken, her children went back inside to eat and rest. It was after a couple of moments that Ms. Shabah herself would walk back inside to tell her kids exactly what she was going to do.

"The first thing I am going to say is that I am beyond disgusted with her. I almost was at the level of friendship where I could invite her to my house for coffee or tea, where we could go picnicking, where we could go for walks around the neighborhood as I did with the graceful and heavily missed Ms. Kabila! I was enjoying her company, even though it was a little strange, and I think everyone else would enjoy her company too. She seemed unproblematic, tranquil with her attitude, and wispy with her language, but obviously, that is wrong. What she did to me is completely unforgivable. I will never speak to that woman again, and I hope you know that. But what I am going to do is going to punish and embarrass her, for I cannot let her go unpunished and unembarrassed. When I was younger, there was this boy that lived next door to me. I was about five or six years old around this time, and I was utterly in love with him; I thought he was the dreamiest little boy ever. He was tan and dark, had the curliest hair, and was slim and slender. He also had the deepest voice of any person in the entire neighborhood, and the entire town. Since we lived next to each other, I would constantly go over to his house, and we would play games together and mess around, and do everything until it was dark and it was time to go home. I only hung around because I wanted him to like me, and one day he did

112

confess that he was indeed in love with me. Each day, I used to ask my mother if she could bring their entire family over for lunch, and that is when I would see him. We used to play outside and see how many moths we could catch. It was a really fun game. Anyways, one day, they came over for lunch as I insisted they do, and I overheard his mother talking to my mother about his day at school. He had apparently proposed to another girl at the school, and they got married. Obviously, that is just some childish, wild imagination that all children have, but it truly hurt me to hear, so I did not spend time with him outside at all for the rest of the day. I then got a poster board that I had found in my mother's office and used it to write a message to him. It wrote, 'Liar. Never come here again' on it, and I put it on the ground on our grass at the front of the house so that it faced his. He never came back and bothered me again, and I believe that the sign was the most effective thing I had ever done. Not only did he not see me again, but his mother made sure that he did not because she found out I had been played by his terrible habits. That is what I am going to do to her. I am going to make sure that she never bothers me again, and I am going to make certain that the entire neighborhood knows of her social crime."

"Mother, that is genius. I love your thinking," said Gabriel. He always respected his mother's thoughts, even if they did not agree with his own.

"Don't you think that might be a little too harsh? I mean, Jason and I—"

"No, Cassandra! It is not too harsh. In fact, the boy not telling you immediately says so many things. You will not see him again. No discussion," yelled the mother.

"But, mother, you cannot do such a thing! We have been so close since we moved here, and he makes me so much happier—" Cassandra was cut off.

"No! No more! Enough!"

Cassandra did not speak again, but her eyes filled with water, drowning her vision. She inhaled sharply and frowned slightly, but then quickly got up to go to her room. She did not slam the door or walk in a quick manner, but simply strolled to her room. The ban from the boy was going to ruin her, but she did not know it yet.

Later that evening, Ms. Shabah took a small mallet and some stakes and hammered her sign into the ground in her front yard closest to the Grealm household. It read, "Dirty woman! Ungodly tart! Never come here again." Ms. Shabah was serious about never talking to her not talk about this but living here is not enjoyable at all. I mean, there is nothing interesting that ever happens in this town, save the annual hopscotch tournament, but seldom that, we are left in nothing but a cool breeze and some basic houses."

"I think you are wrong. In Fiddlefield, there was nothing like this. Quintbridge is a wonder of the world compared to most places— maybe it is just your privileges seeping through your mind. Everyone who grows up in a place they have known their entire lives will do nothing but loathe their place, even if it is a palace to other people. Perhaps that is why you hate it so much," said Gabriel.

"Yes, but how can we not hate it if this is the place you are describing in your theory?" asked the youngest Ledger. It was quite thoughtful for someone who was only around the age of fourteen.

"Well, yes, I suppose so," said Andra now. "In my opinion, I think it is almost impossible to take the philosophy that Gabriel said and apply it to your own lives. It does not mean that it is wrong, though, because what Gabriel said is very correct, but all you need to do is experience insignificance. That is the only way you can appreciate what you have—when you take yourself out of the existence of your own world and put it to the side to just watch everything in the eyes of a bystander. That lack of insignificance is the sole reason that many believe their lives are so terrible and contribute to the ungratefulness of mankind. It is what creates such high standards, not just for life, but for love too. However, there are only a small handful of people who have actually managed to attain that level of humility. At least that is what I read once."

"Wow, sister, I am impressed! Who knew you had such intellect hidden in that very small brain of yours," said Gabriel jokingly. The rest of the boys laughed along with him, taking the heavy seriousness of the conversation to something lighter. "Shut it, Gabriel!" said her, also smiling with his sarcasm.

A full hour went by once the Shabahs realized that Cassandra Farrow was not likely to show up at the edge of the pond. All of them wondered if the Lillis twins had been lying to them—being mischievous little boys just for fun—but it did not matter to them if they were or not. The Shabah siblings decided to leave, bidding the boys goodbye. They were incredibly good company, and their presence was so soothing—it was as if the siblings enter a state of tranquility when talking to them about meaningless subjects out of a teenager's control—and the siblings again and refused to interact with her. When people walked by, it was like there was a monument standing, and they would stop and stare. For Ms. Shabah, it was entirely worth it, and she believed that the woman needed to remember where she stood in the composition of the neighborhood. It was not worth prostituting yourself for some attention, and if Bonnie Grealm truly needed some sort of attention, she could have received it from somewhere else. Ms. Shabah watched everyone walk by the house through the windows for some time but then moved to the study, where she found her children reading through some papers and books. She addressed them with command.

"Andra and Gabriel, I am going to have the Victoriana couple over for dinner, and we will be discussing a few things about this neighborhood. I want it to be a private conversation, which means you both need to find somewhere else to go. Cassandra, you will not go to the Grealm household; you will never go to the Grealm household. If I find you did, I am going to send you to the other side of the country to live alone in a boarding school. Do not go there. Find somewhere to go in this neighborhood, not more than a ten-minute walk from this very house," she said instructively.

"Yes, mother, that is actually perfect. You see, there is a bonfire tonight by the pond—I had just received news of it from the Ledger brothers—and we would love to go. Cassandra and I can go together, and we won't make any problems. We can be back at the house later tonight," said Gabriel.

"How did you hear news of it, brother?"

"None of your business, Andra. Stop asking stupid questions."

"Don't be rude, brother," she said, offended at his comment.

"No more talking. Leave, both of you, now," demanded their mother. She had become extremely distressed at her situation, and she wanted her children gone, somewhere where they could not disturb her any further. She did love them and wish the best for their futures and current lives, but she could no longer stand their presence with hers.

Gabriel and Andra left immediately, making their trek to the campfire by the emerald lake. It was quiet outside, but they felt like the entire world was surrounding them during that moment and could not help but feel an annoying itch on their back that they could not satisfy, no matter how they squirmed and flailed. Once they got to the fire, they realized why they had felt this way and had sensed, far in advance, something that was going to alter the outcome of the course tonight.

The Ledger boys were seated along the logs of the campfire, their legs spread lazily and arms holding on to the thick pieces of bark. They were talking in slurs, speaking as if they could not control the sloppy manner of their tongue. On the ground in front of them, a keg was standing, and each of them had cups in their hands filled with a mysterious liquid that looked clear and brown at the same time. It was alcohol. Andra had never seen alcohol before and felt compelled to have at least a single sip, but was very quickly shut down by her brother, who knew exactly what she was thinking.

"Absolutely not, Andra. Don't even think about it. I can practically hear your thoughts. Alcohol is completely off-limits for you," he said quite firmly.

"I wasn't even thinking about it," she replied in a whiny tone, rolling her eyes as she made her way to the edge of a log to sit down.

"Don't lie to me, sister. I know you better than you know yourself." He sat in between the boys, who poured him a cup gladly.

"How come you get to drink some, but I can't? That is not far, Gabriel!"

"Oh, just shut up. Your lover is coming here. If you complain about not being allowed to drink again, I am going to tell our mother about you hanging with the boy. How would you like that?"

"If you tell her I am going to kill you. Oh, I hate you! I hate you so much at this moment!" She sounded like she was sulking on the log and Gabriel could not stand it. He felt more annoyed by her presence than at any time before.

Within a few minutes, Gabriel was feeling drowsy and weird. He started to slur his words, drool, and act like a sloppy mess. Cassandra found it disgusting and did not want to stay at the bonfire any longer; all she wished to do was go home and sleep in her bed, desiring her boy—who she was banished from seeing—to be in the same bed as her. Gabriel was falling on the Ledger boys, embarrassing himself for his failure to maintain his stature. The first taste of alcohol made him gag, but as he attempted to prove himself superior to the other boys by continuously drinking the alcohol, he began to let loose and become a different person. His breath reeked of the sour, ham-like smell of alcohol, and he made his sister repulse when he talked too close to her face. She could not understand this sudden change in his personality— from the tender essence of a brother to a troublesome stranger, ready to yell and scream and cause a fit. She felt like she could no longer relate to her brother at this very moment, especially since knowing how he stabbed her in the back when talking to their mother, when he mentioned how he was going to inform their mother of Jason and her spending time together, and when he had a random, extreme resistance to alcohol when she asked to try some.

After a short period of time, Jason appeared and sat next to Cassandra immediately, saving her from listening to the drunken boys any longer. He seemed exhausted from the day and exhaled quite loudly as he sat down. The sweet smell of lavender coming from Cassandra's long, brown hair intoxicated him, and he pulled her in closer while the fire flickered in front of them. They very quickly came to realize that they did not enjoy how silly the boys had gotten, and Andra still retained some of the anger that her brother had caused her to have. Still, they sat at peace with one another, not speaking until Andra decided it was time to start a conversation.

"Do you want to hear about my day, my sweet?" she asked Jason.

"Of course, Andra. Tell me," he insisted.

"Well, there has been a huge change. After my mother found out about the fact that your mother slept with Popov, she had become quite angry, obviously, and set a boundary against us. She doesn't want me to ever see you again, which I will not accept because I love to be around you. I think the situation is quite ridiculous, and I cannot wait for this whole problem to be over. It has made my relationship with my other quite worse, and," she said, slowly lowering her voice to an almost whisper, "it has made my relationship with my brother awful. I do not know what has possessed him, but he has become extremely rude. I want him to relax a little bit more, but he won't, and keeps irritating me with the supreme rules that he likes to enforce. You know, he is saying I cannot even try the alcohol—not that I wanted to, but I cannot even if I did. It just seems like our relationship is deteriorating. My mother, on the other hand, has also become extremely irritable, but for an actual reason. She is saying that, since she has been in a dispute with your mother, it is disrespectful to continue having any sort of contact with her family, which includes you. I won't do that, however. I refuse—"

"Are you saying something, Cassandra Shabah?" asked Gabriel, interrupting his sister of her gossip.

"I am, but not about you."

"Yes, you are. I heard you, stupid girl." She remained silent for a moment—her eyes swelling with tears—before she stood from the log and began to raise her voice.

"What is your problem, Gabriel? What is it? Tell me, what has made you so angry? Why do you hate me now? Why?" She nearly screamed this to him. He dropped his cup, spilling the brown liquid on the ground, which almost went close to the fire and could have been catastrophic, before standing up and matching the stance of his sister.

"You know what my issue is with you, ignorant girl? I have come to realize over the past few hours that you are entirely annoying. Every action you have ever done is for your selfish good, uncaring about anything or anyone else in the world. You hate Cassandra Farrow for no reason at all, except that she is 'eccentric' and you talk in this complaining voice. Why don't you ever just… talk normally? Just speak normally! You complain and whine and everyone else has to slave to your needs. We all hate you, Cassandra. Everyone does! You manage to anger everyone around you with how you lie and manipulate and think that everyone agrees with your strange thoughts, but that just is not true. No one agrees with you, Cassandra! And if you just managed to shut your mouth about the entire Grealm household situation, there wouldn't be this bizarre mood in the house. Mother wouldn't be so unhappy all the time if you just shut your mouth! I have realized all of this over the past few days, and how everything you have ever said or done was only for the good of yourself. It is the truth, and luckily, I had this amazing beer to help me release my inner thoughts, but that is the truth. That's it."

Everyone remained silent. It was only the awkward shake of the leaves above them, resulting from the endless breeze that streamed through the neighborhood, and the sudden snapping of twigs beneath their feet that made any sort of noise. Cassandra stood with her mouth agape, her eyes shining from the tears that filled them. It was so awkward, in fact, that the Ledger boys couldn't help but turn and look at each other, recognizing the same awkwardness they felt. Witnessing two siblings fighting, especially as viciously as the two just did create a situation that felt utterly uncomfortable.

"And I just would like to add," continued Gabriel, "that Cassandra Farrow, the girl you hate, is still missing. No one has seen her at all. No one even talks about it! It's like she just disappeared in real life and in your memories. This is not just directed at my sister, but all of you. I am just so angry right now. So unbelievably angry at the fact that she has just been annihilated from our conversations. I miss her dearly, and I suppose all of you should miss her too."

Cassandra Shabah sat back down in the middle of his spiel about Cassandra Farrow, without a single word being said except for the loud, gargling voice of her brother. Eventually, once he finished talking, he too sat back down.

From the distance, a bright smile appeared. It was that of Delilah Candella, moving through the grounds outside and avoiding the low-hanging branches of some of the trees. She wore an incredibly light and fluid skirt, the same color as pickles, and a white buttoned shirt. Her hair was put into a bun, resting softly at the top of her intelligent head. She brought with her a buoyant and cheerful mood, bringing the dark and dismal colors of the setting to something more the color of a strawberry or the luscious green grass of the spring. Everyone was particularly excited to see her arrive at the bonfire, except for Cassandra and Jason, who refused to take notice of the girl while they dealt with Cassandra's troubles. She was still recovering from her fight, but Gabriel recovered so easily and quickly as if Delilah snatched his problems and waves of anger from him and burned them until they were nothing but soft smoke that floated into the air.

"Hey everyone. Is this some sort of beer? I remember having my first drink a few years ago. Mind if I take a cup?"

"For sure. Be my guest, Lila," said the eldest Ledger, who gladly filled up a cup of beer for her.

"How do you know that nickname?" asked Gabriel.

"I don't, I suppose. I just said it," replied the boy.

"Don't ever say it again. That is not your nickname to say."

"Gabriel! It is not a big deal if he calls me Lila instead of Delilah," said the girl.

"No! It is our nickname! Our thing. He must not take it from us," said Gabriel.

"Here we go, again. Sensitive Gabriel begins yelling about nonsense," said Cassandra.

"Oh, well now the girl speaks! Let's not do that again," retorted Gabriel.

"That is enough! Both of you! I just arrived here, unrealizing that I had walked in on a dispute. Why can't we enjoy our time together without any of this nonsense ruining things? Please, all of you, stop. And just to reiterate, *anyone* can call me Lila if they so please."

Once they began adjusting to a better environment, where the toxicity of sensitivity no longer ruined the atmosphere, the bonfire crew became happier. They joked more instead of yelling about nothing, and

Gabriel lightened up from his angry attitude. However, they soon heard a gruff grunt from the woods and the quick stepping on twigs that sounded like a sprint. Wide-eyed and fearful, the group stood up, focusing deeply in the dark of the woods to see who—or what—could be attempting to come over to them.

CHAPTER XX

"Thank you for coming, Florence and Granger. I truly appreciate it," said Ms. Shabah. The couple sauntered inside the home, wandering around before stumbling to the dining room. They were wearing the same clothes they had been wearing since they reached their level of homelessness. There was a deeply unsettling, raunchy stench coming from their clothes—resulting from the lakes of sweat that had swelled and contaminated their clothes and skin—and there was a small trail of dusty soil following them inside.

"If it isn't too much trouble, my dear Victorianas, I would appreciate it if you took a bath. I have two upstairs that you could use, but you both do not smell good whatsoever. I understand your situation, and I am aware of what I said could have been perceived as rude, but I want this to be dinner as if you were in the same home. We have a lot to discuss, and I would love you both to be my guests and make yourselves feel as if you were in your home. I know it is a little bit strange and bizarre, but this is what I ask. We are classy individuals, and so we must dress like it always."

The couple looked at each other, feeling the string of arrogance from the Shabah woman wrap around them tightly. However, they did desperately need a shower and took the chance to clean up temporarily while they still can. After all, they were aware of their physical state—as were all the homeless—and were aware of the impact it had on people around them. They asked Ms. Shabah if they could wear some of the clothes she had, which she acquiesced to, except that she was sure there might be something large enough for Granger to wear in Gabriel's closet.

The freshening scent of perfume floated down the steps towards the grandeur of the dining room, where Ms. Shabah sat patiently for them to arrive back after a long forty minutes. Florence wore a tight, pink dress that she borrowed from Ms. Shabah's closet, fitting her perfectly. She accompanied it with some jewelry that she already wore, whose silver complexion complimented the dress nicely. Her hair, still damp and dark, was tied up, exposing the smooth skin on the back of her neck. Granger found some pants from Gabriel's wardrobe, which fit him tightly, but suited him well, and then a shirt that was quite large. He assumed that it was an inherited shirt from his father, but obviously could not be sure.

On the dining table was a platter of foods that could be devoured over a series of days and still not be finished. On the end closest to Ms. Shabah was a large turkey, and next to that was a ham, which stood next to a giant bowl of salad, and then some potatoes, a pie, three bowls of pudding, a warm tray of carrots that had been roasted, some bread and butter, and finally some strawberries and cream, a delicious dessert that was a favorite of the Shabah household.

"Is this meant to be eaten by all of us?" asked Florence, sparkling in her glamorous dress.

"As I had just said, we have a lot to discuss," replied the woman.

"Did you cook all of this yourself?"

"Yes, of course. I have never had someone else prepare food for me. Food is the love of life; when I give you food, it is my way of expressing my love for you. Now, we must begin this feast! I am excited to begin eating, and I need to get started talking. Let's start by passing out the food and then talk from there."

The food went around in a circle, and only after the third or fourth dish, the plates were full. They were unsure of what to do, but Ms. Shabah assured them that they could just eat the rest after they finished the table. She was asserting the fact that all of her food was to be shared in whatever amounts permissible by them, and that they should be encouraged to eat well tonight.

"Well, while you both feast on the meats and the starches, I am going to lick on the strawberries and cream, as well as the pies, and begin talking," said Ms. Shabah. There was the sound of licking and eating before she began to speak with a half-full mouth, leaking strawberries from the corners of her lips. "What I really wanted to discuss was that wretched woman on the side of me: that ugly Bonnie Grealm. She has totally disgraced me and my family's name."

She took a break from speaking—it had only been a few seconds—and began eating slices of her pie. "In what way, Ms. Shabah?" asked Granger, seeming to want to hear the rest of the conversation.

"Well, she was caught sleeping with that miserable Russian. It is just so disgusting how she decided to sleep with that man, of all men in this gross neighborhood. I am seriously angry with her. The way that

I found out was from my daughter, who went to visit the boy there. She walked inside and witnessed the woman and the Russian 'bedding' together. It made me physically ill. Listen, I don't want you to associate yourselves with that woman ever again. Also, I put up a sign in my front yard that basically cursed her and her family's name because of that. Keep in mind, he literally slept with my daughter."

The Victoriana couple was deeply puzzled. "I'm sorry, excuse me? He slept with your daughter?" asked Florence.

"No! God, no! I meant to say that he ruined my daughter's life. He practically tried to get her placed in jail, and at her age! When I say he is a miserable man, I truly mean it."

"I am going to be honest with you, lovely Ms. Shabah, but you are making no sense at the moment. It is quite scrambled—the way you talk of these events. Tell them to us in deep detail," stated Granger. Ms. Shabah explained the events in a description that was particularly expounded, trying to analyze the meaning and motives behind each move that Bonnie Grealm had done. When she was finished, the Victoriana couple was shocked, as if lightning had struck through their bodies and left them fragilely still and stuck.

A sudden knock was at the front door. It had been only an hour of gossiping about the woman next door, but Ms. Shabah excused herself and got up to go to the front door. Upon opening it, she noticed that there was nobody present to greet her, but rather a small letter was placed in front of the door. She immediately knew what was present in her hands, and her stomach dropped at the thought of what it could read.

"Granger and Florence Victoriana, you will not believe what I have in my hand right now," said Ms. Shabah, holding the letter behind her back to purposefully obscure it from their view.

"I assume it is some sort of package. Perhaps even some more delicious food, delivered from the kindness of the neighbors?" thought Granger.

"What if it is a note by the police for our arrest, Granger? We are the homeless that have infested the neighborhood. Oh, God!" exclaimed Florence. The couple seemed both startled and terrified by what could be behind the back of Ms. Shabah.

"No, you two. It is simply the devil herself. She has written another letter! Carol Farrow, after all this time of not speaking at all, has finally delivered me a letter!"

"Well, quickly come sit down and read it!" hurried Florence.

"Alright, I shall. Let's see."

Dearest Neighbors,

I am finally writing another one of my splendid letters. I have missed this! Well, it has been quite some time since I have released another incredible piece of journalism to you all, but here I am, finally.

It appears that the kind Lady Grealm has been caught sleeping with the Russian man, Popov. How disgusting. The one woman who has made such a big deal out of it all is the woman across the street, the one with the child murderer, and the one helping the homeless freakshow that lives underground in their old house: Ms. Shabah. How the woman continues to disappoint is beyond me! However, there is a secret that she, along with some other women in this neighborhood, is not telling you.

Ms. Shabah, as well as Lady Victoriana, Ms. Kabila (may her soul rest, although she was a putrid lady), the four women that live in the house by the lake, the elderly woman who is married to the man with the horse, the lady with eleven cats, and, of course, Lady Grealm have all slept with the man. In fact, it is so ridiculous that Ms. Shabah even makes this a big deal, considering that she has already slept with him and has only been here a few weeks.

Popov had tried to sleep with me, but obviously, his attempts failed. I will never be sleeping with a man who has attained that level of disgust and revolt, unlike the rest of the women here. Also, just to make sure you all know, he is diseased!

Good luck, idiot of a woman.

Carol Farrow

There was both a brief and infinite moment of silence at the dining table before Granger erupted into a fit of anger.

"Excuse me? You and that disgusting Popov? Is that true?" he asked her, voice infuriated and angry at the rumor he had just heard. His bushy eyebrows pointed downward, and his mouth had a slight downturn. It felt as if the heat radiating from his irate body was evaporating the water in front of him as it swished in its cup from the shaking of his leg.

"No, Granger, of course not. I would never do that, and you know that."

"Well, why else, Florence, would she claim that you have slept with him? As far as we know, you were the closest out of anyone else to her and she turned on you only from our... situation, but that does not mean that she didn't tell the truth!"

"Yes, it does, Granger! If anything, she purposefully lied to make us more disagreeable. Granger, darling, believe me. I would never do such a thing, and you know that, especially from what happened the last time I—," she was interrupted.

"Enough of this! Shut up, you gross woman! I cannot believe that this is the second time I have had to deal with a situation like this." When his words boomed against the walls of the dining room, shaking the flames of the candles on the table and rattling the walls, he got up suddenly, picking up a plate of sausage and a bowl of pudding and throwing it at his wife. She gasped quite loudly at the action, and stood up quite suddenly, allowing the pudding to drip further down her dress and the sausage to stain some more sections of the dress.

"Lady Victoriana, please! My dress! Hurry up and take it off upstairs, quickly!" said Ms. Shabah who tried to help the woman get up from her seat. Granger Victoriana was still increasingly frustrated at the situation and did not want the conversation to end.

"No. Sit back down, immediately, you cheating, wretched wife! I cannot believe this of you!"

"Oh, shut up, Granger," responded Ms. Shabah. "You know good and well that what she is saying is nothing but false—a lie. It is always a lie. Now, look at you! You have embarrassed yourself with your irresistible urges to make dramatic fits. It is puny and pathetic how terribly easy it is to fire up you men. Please, clean this mess. Obviously,

Carol is not telling you the truth; she is only speaking to make you mad, and it quite obviously worked."

He seemed stunned at how quickly he was told how wrong he was. He moved to go clean the mess, profusely apologizing while also waddling in hopes of not ripping or tearing the pants of Ms. Shabah's son.

✳   ✳   ✳

"Listen, I really do believe that it is best if you both just go back to where you were. I will handle this problem with the Farrow woman, and trust me, she will be handled—but you must go back. I feel like this entire circumstance, at the moment, has turned into something that was not originally intended to be. Thank you both for coming, I appreciate it very much, and I can clean up from here. Thank you. Goodnight now!" said Ms. Shabah in her kindest and most tired voice.

She left the dining table as it was and went immediately toward the study. She pulled a blank piece of paper from a desk, along with a pen and some ink to dip it in. She decided to write her own letter, one that would combat each of the claims that Lady Farrow preached were true and one that played her same game. She scribbled relentlessly for almost thirty minutes before she reached her final draft.

> My dearest neighbors,
> It is time that someone acts out against this woman. She had done enough terrorizing this neighborhood, and when she gets called out on it, she acts as if she is Marie Antoinette: stupid. I am personally sick of Lady Carol Farrow being allowed to write letters to each of you, and so, in the fashion of Her Grace, I am going to be writing a letter in refuting.
> Let me begin with the first and most important claim: my daughter is not a child murderer. She has never harmed a living organism in her entire life, and for any of you to think as if she had anything to do with the depressing, premature,

undeserving death of the lovely and forever memorable Ms. Kabila, you must be crazy.

Secondly, I think we have had enough of the accusations. Lady Farrow has constantly accused people of criminal, shameful activity that they had never done. Recently, it has come to my attention that there was a letter written about many other ladies and myself and that we had slept with that disgusting Russian. Although I cannot speak for the rest, I do know that Lady Victoriana, Ms. Kabila, and I had never slept with this man. I am not sure how many other women are as innocent as myself, but I am sure that it is more than only us three. I was shocked to find out that we had been accused of prostituting ourselves to a miserable, crazed man like Popov.

Finally, I would like to address the fact that I believe Lady Farrow to be utterly insane. How else would someone find the time to consume themselves with other people's lives in order to feel satisfied that something interesting is happening in their lives? How else does someone believe that their lives are filled with dramatic and wonderful things when, in reality, there are not? I will not say that I am claiming a fact, but my hypothesis is strongly recommended as being true both philosophically and logically. No woman should ever have the time to do anything other than their regular housework, especially if they have children, which we know Lady Farrow does, indeed, have.

I want to end this letter by ending all letters. There should never be a discussion between people about a subject in which they know nothing. Why continue discussing when we can halt and live happily? Happiness should be enough to suffice the voids in our lives, not drama.

Goodnight, my dearest neighbors,
Shabah Household

She quickly rushed to the Victoriana couple who still lay outside beneath the house of the two best friends. She needed their advice about the letter and in what fashion she should deliver it, considering the Victoriana Household was one of the oldest and most respected when it was present.

"May you proofread my letter? I had written it to the Farrow woman in hopes to attack what she has been saying, but I want it to come off as mature. What do you think?" asked Ms. Shabah to the Victoriana woman.

She waited a moment, awkwardly standing in the whispers of the breeze while Florence read the letter. She turned to the woman once she was finished. Ms. Shabah was eager to receive her feedback but was unsure as to how she might perceive the letter. Florence's eyes began to water, slowly dripping as she handed back the letter.

"It's perfect, Ms. Shabah. Absolutely perfect," was all she managed to say. She smiled and cried, hugging her poor husband who seemed delighted at the fact that someone was finally disgracing Lady Farrow after all this time.

Ms. Shabah grabbed some other pieces of paper, writing down the exact copy of the letter on each so that she could deliver them to multiple houses. She felt as if she was going to move people with this letter, and every paper she filled with her paragraphs of rebellion filled her with joy.

She completed twenty pieces of paper—each detailing the reasons why Lady Farrow was bringing this neighborhood to its demise. In the depths of the evening, when the moon was high and the night was blindingly dark, she walked outside to the mailboxes surrounding her. She put a letter in each, rang the doorbells—or knocked if there was no doorbell already installed—and carried on down the street until there were no more letters to hand out. Once she was finished, she felt compelled to wait for the responses from people, and it wasn't until an hour later that she heard the first of many knocks on her door concerning the letter.

CHAPTER XXI

The silhouette of a stranger was shifting between the trees and bushes that stood between it and the group. It was weaving left and right rapidly, breathing heavier, and slowly approaching. Cassandra began to scream fearfully and took some steps back toward the pond. Gabriel and the Ledger boys hushed her, but it did not matter; the stranger was bound to have already heard her screams. She was certain it was Popov, coming to their group to snatch one of the children and put them on display for public humiliation, or worse, murder them as the rumor goes.

The group stopped fearing what was lurking ahead of them once they realized there was a flowy white dress moving between the bushes and the branches. It was that of Cassandra Farrow's, elegantly moving through the wind. Her face was perfectly clear save for the few scars underneath her eyes that glowed a soft pink. She seemed vibrant, well-rested, and assured. Her confidence in her strides seemed to sponge the attention of the group, hypnotizing them as if a great beauty had walked by them.

"Hello, everyone," she said calmly. She looked at everyone in a panorama, individually making eye contact with each person in her sight so that she could acknowledge their presence and maintain their focus.

"You are here. In your own flesh, Cassandra," said Gabriel, shocked at her appearance. Cassandra had not been seen in many days, and the last time they had even heard of the poor girl, it was in a rumor of abuse and blood. She had gone missing, and no one seemed to notice.

"Yes, I am. I am back for now. There is a lot I must tell you all. You must sit down again."

"Why are you back? No disrespect, I just wonder what you are doing here, in the middle of the woods, in a dress, like you are all glamoured up for us to see," asked Andra.

"Shut your mouth, girl. Do not speak for the rest of the time," said her brother. She only looked on in silence, as everyone stared at her. She felt very embarrassed. It was a disgusting comment she should not have needed to make, and she felt everyone's disdain for her comment. Everyone knew she wasn't particularly fond of Cassandra Farrow, but she continued to do as she asked, and sat next to Jason.

The logs were stationed in a triangular shape. On a single log sat Cassandra Farrow, putting one leg over her other. She sat with her dress tucked underneath herself and straightened out the folds with the brush of her hands. On the log to her left sat Gabriel and Delilah, furthest away from her, and the eldest three Ledger boys. Each of them was holding a cup filled with the brown liquid they prepared beforehand. They reeked an awful lot. The last log had only Andra and Jason, both sitting on the edge furthest from Cassandra Shabah. Andra sat straight and uptight, watching the girl with a glare, waiting for her to begin speaking.

Following a deep inhale, Cassandra Farrow began talking.

"I must confess that my sudden disappearance was dramatic; it created quite a stir in this community. However, there was a reason for all of that. As some of you might have guessed if you heard the circling rumors about me, I was terribly abused by my mother. This scar next to my left eye came from her long fingernail when she slapped me across the face. It pierced my skin and left me bleeding. Under my eye was my sister, Fabiana, who was instructed by my mother to beat me since I got caught sneaking out to go see you, Gabriel. The scar that you cannot see since it is hidden behind my hairline, came from the time my mother took my head in her hands and slammed me into a corner of the table. That was when I was five years old. There are a handful of other scars as well, all from similar actions, and some burns as well, mostly from boiling water or just really hot water—not exactly boiling. They accumulated on my body, lines of memories from the times when my mother hurt me most. I share with you all this vulnerable side of me, one where I am not the eccentric girl who laughs in at each joke or over-explains the small events in my life that give me joy, or scrapbooks in my free time from the windowsill."

"However, over the recent time that I spent away from all of you, I have decided to keep my thoughts generating in a calm state, away from my family and with only myself. While I sat there thinking, I realized that I needed to do something about my situation. My mother and my siblings do not love me. I am alone in this world, only boosted by a family so that they could seem like they are making a change for me when in reality, I am suffering. I do not look like the Farrow family. I am alone. But I shan't accept this fate of mine, and I needed to make a change, so I did exactly that." Cassandra Farrow pulled a small piece of paper out from her right pocket and unfolded it. There were many scribbled words and arrows blotted on the paper, and she stared at it intensely. Her hands shook, and she certainly could not read the material, but she did not look up. The silence of the group as they heard the faint splash of a tear from her eye on the corner of the paper. Soon, there were three more droplets, sounding like the very ending of a strong shower where only a couple of heavy water drops make an impact. She stood up and faced the group again; her eyes were clear and there was no stream of tears on her face whatsoever.

"Here. This is what I am going to do. Just as my awful mother does to people who irritate her, I shall do the same. This is the brief outline of a letter I am to write to this neighborhood, detailing each and every circumstance and event that navigated their way to impact my life as well as the familiar dynamic of my household. I thought I should read it to you all before I am to write it, and I was going to ask if you could possibly help me with some of the material, since it will be impossible to complete this letter and spread it on my own. I am going to begin with a historical account of my adoptive mother, and how she came to adopt, the relationship with my adoptive father, how they divorced, and everything else that has happened that led to this day. After that, I am going to explain some of the things my mother has done to me, as well as my siblings, what my siblings have done, and my plans for my future. I think it's set up perfectly. What do you guys think?"

"Well, are we going to get more details on what exactly you mean by history, plans, your siblings, and everything else?" asked the eldest Ledger boy.

"Yes, I am planning on it. I feel as if, given I have some hours of spare time, I can write the entire story in one sitting. Anything else?" she asked.

There was a brief moment of silence, but everyone knew who was going to ask the next question. A slight stutter to breathe and begin talking exposed Gabriel's intention to speak, and every head turned in his direction. He gave up trying to think of whatever sentence would help elicit his ideas kindlier and exhaled sharply. "Don't you think you are being a hypocrite?"

"What do you mean, Gabriel? I haven't said anything that seems hypocritical," replied the girl.

"Yes, actually, you have. You are writing a letter exposing deep and sensitive parts of your family's life, just as your mother does when she is talking about other people in her letters. I mean, you are literally writing a *letter*. You are copying her exact method of breaking the news, and everyone hates her method. Why would you do that?"

"Do you not think that I know this information? I'm very much aware. I am simply playing her game, Gabriel. Do you think I should just let her do whatever she pleases for longer?"

"No, that is not what I mean when I say—"

"Yes, it is what you mean! You do not support me in this! I cannot believe you."

"I did not say that!"

"I think what he means," said Delilah, "is that he thinks you are going to be seen just like your mother: a wretched human being. I think he wants you to realize that you might be hurting your image if you write a letter that practically exposes your entire family."

"Lila, I do not need you to articulate on my behalf," said Gabriel, frustrated and offended at Cassandra's claims.

"But it is true! Am I wrong for saying this?" she asked Gabriel.

"No, but I do not need you to speak to her as if you are me," he said to Delilah.

"Her? You mean the girl who is standing write here?" Cassandra bitterly asked. "Am I invisible to you? Am I not making sense when I say that you are not supporting me entirely? Do you need your stupid girlfriend to tell me what you mean because you cannot say it yourself? Have you forgotten who brought you two together in the first place? I certainly have not, and I highly encourage you to realize the situation and stop playing the antagonist for a minute."

"That isn't what we mean, Cassandra. I only want to extend his argument, which is that it *is* hypocritical in nature. You are only destroying yourself by writing such a thing," said Delilah.

"Do you genuinely think I care about my public image right now, Delilah?" she said furiously. The white in her eye shined ever-so-brightly in the light of the fire. They dammed with water, streaming some tears down her face as she stood in shock at the girl's comment. She was so angry that the air seemed to burn red with fury, and each person was uncomfortable as if they were sitting on a plank of needles. Now she was screaming, yelling as if no one around her could hear or understand.

"Do you seriously think I care? Huh? Are you going to answer me, you dumb half-brain of a girl?" There was nothing that was said, only the acceptance of the scrutiny that Cassandra unleashed as she stood. Everyone watched her as she continued to scream. "No, you are not going to answer me, because I am not wrong. I have scars on my whole face, and you sit here, and truly believe that I am going to ruin my public image! As if I care what you have to say! If it wasn't abundantly clear, your opinion means nothing to me. You all sit here and soak my life up as if the dramatic events that happen fulfill your existence. I will not accept it. I thought you were my friend, Delilah, and now I am hearing your stupid thoughts come out of your stupid mouth and believe that your stupid comments are helping me from making stupid decisions. I am doing whatever I want, and I do not care what any of you have to say about it. I thought if I informed you earlier, you wouldn't be as concerned when it came out on its own."

"I am sorry, Cassandra. We did not know—"

"Look! You are doing it again, Delilah. 'We.' You say it as if he does not have a voice. Speak, you ignorant boy! Speak! Apologize to me!"

"I am sorry, Cassandra," he muttered.

"I think it is best if you do not speak to my brother this way, Cassandra," said Gabriel's sister, slowly rising from her seat at the log, stern in her expression.

"Oh, you shut your mouth, or I will slit your throat and make sure you do not speak again! I know your hatred for me, and I have felt it since the first day. I am not socially ignorant. If it was legal and there were no repercussions, I would rip your hair out of your skull and burn it as you scream in pain. Now shut your mouth." Cassandra Shabah closed her mouth and sat back down.

"Gabriel," continued Cassandra Farrow, "I have loved you for a while. Has it not been so obvious? I tried as much as I could to let it be known, but… never mind. I know that you now love Delilah, and that's fine. However, I do ask that you not question the ethical standpoint of my actions, because, at this point, I do not care. I don't even want to care; I only wish to get the justice I deserve. Now, I ask the rest of you, are you going to help me or not? That is the only question I want to hear an answer to."

"Yes," said the eldest Ledger. "Our father has a printing press in the house because of the business, so we can help you once you are ready for the letter to distribute."

"I will not be helping in this matter. Same with Jason," said Andra.

"Luckily for you, I do not care about your help," said Cassandra in retortion. "How about you both?"

133

Gabriel and Delilah sat in silence before Gabriel spoke. "We can read it before you send it out, but we must not get too involved because of my mother—and Delilah's mother."

"Well, then. I guess my work here is completed. It was nice to see these familiar faces after such a long period of time, and I appreciate all the kindness you all have shown me." She glared directly at Delilah and Andra. "The Lillis twins are going to get me now. I will see you all very soon."

"I have a question for the twins when they come here," mentioned the eldest Ledger. Very shortly, the twins showed up and helped Cassandra avoid the bushed and thorns in the forest. The Ledger stood quickly to ask the boys. "Why did Popov chase you over the quarry of rocks on the other side of the pond? I have wanted to know for a long time since I saw it happen."

"Well, he chased us 'round the water 'cause he wanted to get us. We caught him in a prollem. His dog always peed on the house he visited most, and it happened to be the women he slept with. Includin' the Grealm woman and a few others. Bye now. We mus' leave." said Connor Lillis. They left after he spoke, disappearing in the thick brush and the wooded land.

Soon after, the Ledgers went back to their home, and Jason left with them. Delilah hugged Gabriel tightly and turned around to go to her home, fading with the darkness of the night. Gabriel and Andra walked back to their house without speaking another word. It was decided that they will be helping her after all, even though her hostile behavior seemed to nauseate them.

They walked back inside. Andra went to her room and closed the door subtly. She did not want to be disturbed but felt as if some solace will help her, although she refused to admit it. She snuggled up to her covers, embracing the soft sheets that she was so familiar with. The amplifying warmth felt comfortable to her, and she felt as if she could never leave her bed when she fell inside. It offered her a commiseration unlike anything else. Gabriel walked into the room and sat beside her on her bed, feeling concerned and apprehensive about what his sister would possibly do. Cassandra bothered her with her comment, and he felt as if he needed to mediate the situation. "It isn't her fault, really. She's been through a lot more than we could imagine, and she has suffered more than anyone else in this neighborhood."

"I know, Gabriel."

"Well... what are you feeling?"

"I feel nothing."

"Andra, she definitely did not mean it. Cassandra does not have the guts to slit a throat, let alone of the man that she supposedly loves."

"Man? Do you consider yourself a man seriously? If you were truly a man, you wouldn't let some ignorant girl with a serious attitude issue say the things that she said. No one should ever speak like that to anyone—ever. You let it happen—to your sister. How embarrassing, Gabriel."

"Andra, I did not interfere because she was about to kill me. She was so furious for some reason that, if I interfered with what she was saying, she would practically snap my neck."

"Great! Fantastic thinking, Gabriel!" she exclaimed sarcastically. She sat back up and smiled at him. "I guess all my problems with you are solved! Since you are so afraid of a girl half your size, who was practically crying over the fact that we said her ideas could come off negatively, I guess it gives you an excuse to act like a clueless baby!"

"I am serious, Andra."

"Do you seriously think that is a valid excuse?"

"Yes, I do. If you were in my position, I think you would understand, too."

"Yes, if I were in a *man's* position, I would understand clearly. Listen, I am not trying to be dramatic here. She told me she was going to slit my throat if I spoke another word. I could probably get her passed as clinically insane. You involuntarily defended her by not speaking up about her cruel treatment."

"She has been through a lot, Andra. A lot more than most people."

"No, she hasn't! That is the thing you don't understand, Gabriel. She has not been through more than most regular people. The 'regular' people you meet are all like her: rich, unworried, inexperienced, and spoiled. They live the easiest lives possible, and now that one has a single fault, they are given the time of the world when there are so many other cases of this happening with actual regular people. I am not giving her a justification for her words and actions. She screamed like a maniac, so I am going to treat her like a maniac. My point is settled."

"Andra, you fail to understand that the difference between all of this is that just because she is experiencing something that many other people face does not mean her experience is invalid. She is the only person, as far as I'm concerned, who is facing circumstances like abuse and violence. Sorry if I am going to rationalize her actions, but I am."

"As I said, my point is settled. I do not wish to speak any further on this subject. Goodnight Gabriel."

"Fine. Be that way. You'll always be stubborn. Goodnight." Gabriel stomped his way out of the room, closed the door, and went back to his room. His breath still smelled of alcohol, and his clothes were sticky and damp, but he drifted to sleep on his bed. The only benefit of this was that his frustration couldn't be perceived when his face was so serene and angel-like. It was as if he was a newborn again, appreciative and in wonderment of the world.

CHAPTER XXII

A small slip of paper, about the size of a large caterpillar native to the neighborhood that was birthed in the earliest days of August, had appeared in the mailboxes of the Shabah, Ledger, Candella, and Grealm households. It was addressed to each of the members who had promised to aid Cassandra Shabah in her quest to destroy her own home: Gabriel and Andra, Jason, all the Ledger boys, and Delilah.

It has Cassandra's delicate handwriting on it, scribbling a small map of the pond area and a couple of paragraphs that represented an idea of what she hopes to present to them. It was dated a week after their last conversation, and she was keen on deliberating about the letter she had written.

> Hello friends,
> I have written my letter in its entirety, and I hope to read it all to you tonight. Meet me in our old area: the triangle. I will be there with the twins and read you my letter. I do not want edit suggestions, but only a reaction. I want to know how it makes you feel.
> Thank you for your help. I know that this mania I am in causes me to be unrelatable and disagreeable but know that I am truly appreciative.
> Cassandra

Andra tried to persuade her brother that they should not go, but he reminded her of their obligation to help. After all, Cassandra was the first kind face they received upon moving to this neighborhood, so why not help her?

Delilah coaxed her parents into allowing her to leave the house tonight with her soft, cradling voice. She told them that she was going to help Gabriel with his Spanish lessons, as she had been doing since the first night he left his home and went to sleep in her room. She felt extremely guilty for being deceitful to her parents but knew that it would be worthwhile in the end.

The Ledger boys had no problems being able to leave their house, so they appeared earlier than Cassandra and the twins. They decided to keep their alcohol at their house because they felt that if they were to get drunk, their sloppiness would anger Cassandra. Perhaps they were more fearful of the girl than they did admire her.

Jason specifically at the same time as the Shabah siblings left so that he could walk with his girl to the logs. He waited at the window, watching intensely for the movement of a dress of the hair of the girl to make its appearance. Once he saw it, he walked outside as casually as he could, avoiding the drunk behavior of his mother, whom he had not recognized since the incident with the Shabah woman.

Once it was nightfall, each of the children was on their way to the triangle, and the twins were instructed to light a fire. It was still quite warm since the summer months were radiating, but Gabriel thought the fire would help calm a possible negative atmosphere that might arise from this reading. The moon was direct across the pond, seeming to sit just above the trees. Each person sat in the same seat as they had the night a week ago, with Gabriel and Delilah together next to the Ledgers, and Andra next to Jason. The twins sat on their log as well, and Cassandra Farrow stood alone at one log, holding many pieces of paper.

"Hello, everyone. I'm glad to see your faces again. Sorry for possibly offending any of you, specifically Delilah and Gabriel when I ridiculed your relationship," said Cassandra carefully and slowly.

Andra turned to Jason. "She did not apologize to me. Interesting," she whispered.

"As you know, I have completed writing my letter that I will be spreading in the neighborhood with the aid of you all. I, of course, wanted to read this to you all so that you know everything you will be dealing with. I also wanted to warn you: some of the material in this is quite disturbing, and this letter is long. Bear with me. Is everyone ready?"

There were no direct answers that were spoken; only the turning of their heads to focus on what the girl was to read indicated that she should begin. Cassandra cleared her throat and cracked her knuckles. She flicked at the paper to force it upright and took a deep inhale.

138

CHAPTER XXIII

"Hello, all residents who may read this letter. My name is Cassandra Farrow. You may know me as the daughter of the lady who writes all the other letters in the neighborhood: Carol Farrow. I am a popular face in this neighborhood, always conversing with whomever I see fit to talk to and bearing gifts to newcomers in the neighborhood as I have with the Shabah family. You may be increasingly confused as to why I, of all people, am writing a letter to you. The reasons for my doing so are long, extensive, and complex, and I am planning to dive into all of those reasons in this letter. Please read everything that I have written down, for it is the only way that you will grasp a complete understanding of everything my family, including myself, have experienced during all this time. It is going to be in the format of telling the story of how my family has become what it is today, and how the events that led to this particular structure have affected me. This is not necessarily an exposition of everything my family has gone through, but it is something that I must address for my safety. I hope someone can reach out to me once this letter has been distributed, so that I may be able to receive the consolation and help for my dire situation that it desperately needs.

"I must say that it all began when I was first adopted. As you may know, I do not look like the rest of my family, which has caused them to treat me differently. I am sure to believe, however, that the reason for my adoption was to create some sort of public service image that my adoptive mother and father could attain and showcase. When they were amid Russia, on an anthropological excursion through the depths of Siberia, they noticed a small orphanage that was run by a single man. He had children only ages newborn to two years old. This is where I was kept, as a single, cold seven-month-old baby. My mother proclaimed, in her journal that she kept underneath her desk, that I looked like the exact child that people would praise me for adopting; my circumstances were grave enough as a child that I could attract pity from the community we lived in. I, obviously, was not alive during this time so I cannot say my opinion on this matter, but I do believe, from an existential point of view, that it is disgusting to do. It only set up the domino effect for the course of events in my life that would lead to what I am now: bruised, broken, and torn.

"Once back from Russia, my family settled back in their humble home in this great neighborhood of Quintbridge. What my father did not know was that she had also brought something along with her from Russia—not just the small baby. She brought the man that was running the cottage of children with her. She had fallen deeply in love with that man on the trip, and you could probably guess who it is. Popov. However, there was a slight dilemma that was introduced when he promised to come to Quintbridge and buy a home here: his orphanage. What could he do with all these children in the middle of Siberia, where nobody was actively trying to adopt any of them? His answer came with a match, by the advice of my mother. He burned the orphanage down with all the children inside—I presume there were approximately sixty abandoned boys and girls. Perhaps it was a blessing that I was the last of them to be taken, and maybe it was by the grace of the Russian man that I was allowed to live in this world. However, it did not take long at all for my father to realize that the Russian man was following us into our neighborhood, and his first response was not some welcoming feeling that some may presume he would have. It was fear.

"He thought that the man was out to kill his entire family, but that was not the case. It would only take a month for him to catch my mother and Popov sleeping together in their bed, mere weeks before their anniversary of nine years of marriage. All the children, Jacques, the eldest boy, and his younger sister, Blanche, were crying at the fact that their parents had gotten into a fight. I was still too young to understand, and it was not until it was explained to me what 'divorce' meant that I actually understood. My father was extremely upset about what had happened with my mother and that man. He was so angry, in fact, that he demanded another anthropological trip happen. Apparently, my mother had a hand in where he was to go next, considering, I admit, they had done monumental work together on the development of native cultures in the modern age. My mother organized a solo trip for him to travel to the middle of the Brazilian Amazon rainforest, where there exists a tribe untouched by humanity. My father, however, was completely unaware of the cannibalistic nature of the tribe and did not think much of it until he was found days later, eaten alive by a group who was meant to pick him up. Clearly, this was organized by my mother to get rid of the man she no longer cared about. That is not what she told us, however. She mentioned a few blurry descriptions about how he died in a boating accident in the river, and that the savage fish had got to him before anyone else could. Now that I have explained it all, it was obvious how much of a twisted lie it was.

"I know that this information is a complete shock to you all, but rest assured, this is all written in an honest account in the notebook underneath her desk. In my mother's selective handwriting, too, which you all must be familiar with. However, in the next few days, my mother rejoiced as she realized she was pregnant with my father's baby—a final gift of his existence for her to remember him by. Was it my adoptive father's baby, though? Or was it perhaps the result of my mother's disgusting betrayal? I will give you a hint: Fabiana has the same eyes as Popov, and she is the only person in my mother's entire lineage to ever have grey eyes. It is clear as the Quintbridge skies that Fabiana, the youngest child in the wretched Farrow household, was the child of the Russian. My mother made sure to treat her as her blood though, and instead, resented me for my awful behavior and sickening face.

"I would often hear accounts of my mother saying how I deserved to be in Siberia forever, and how she wished I could only speak Russian so that she could never understand what I said and could easily forget that I even spoke. She blamed 'the rotten adoptive girl' for everything wrong in life and encouraged her real children to use me as blame for any problem. However, the true expression of my mother's words happened at the beginning of the new year a few years ago. Carol Farrow, which I will now refer to her since she is no longer a mother to me, sat us down in the living room and explained to Jacques, Blanche, and Fabiana how I was the epitome of evil. Every problem in the house, whether it be the crack in the wall or the financial state of Carol Farrow, was because of the curse that I was. I still remember her words: 'if you want to beat a curse, you must beat the curse.' This meant exactly as she intended to. If you wanted me, the curse, to be gone forever and stop destroying the world that the incredibly superior Farrow household lives in, you must beat and whip and chain and starve the curse until it is gone. After she explained it, she tied me to the trunk of the Christmas tree that we had from a while ago and forced Jacques to kick me as hard as he could. She told him that it was completely my fault that everything bad happened, and instructed the next child, Blanche to kick me. However, she refrained from allowing Fabiana to hurt me because she had other ideas for that child.

"For years, I endured the abuse of Carol Farrow and her children—her *real* children—and felt as if I did not belong. However, each of those feelings would be combatted with other sentiments that she used to tell me. 'Cassandra, you are just as much Farrow as the rest of us,' commonly came out of her mouth, right before she instructed her children to beat and punch and kick, but they only confused me. It felt as if I could never fully determine if I belonged with the rest of them since that is all I've known in my life. My own brothers and sisters would hit me for hours because they felt frustrated at whatever happened in their lives, and Carol Farrow would ask them to beat me when she felt like she had been wronged, but then everything would change moments after when they would say something that would make me feel safe again. Do you see how damaging this was to me? I call upon the people of Quintbridge to help me bring this woman to justice, both for me and my father. However, I am not done yet.

"Popov was beginning to become bored with the monogamous relationship of the Farrow woman and felt as if he needed something else to satisfy him. He first began with one other woman: Bonnie Grealm. However, his impulses were never enough. Carol Farrow knew all of this but continued to allow him to do whatever he pleased. It was embarrassing on her part, but nobody could know! It would destroy the Farrow household's reputation for good! Yet, I know the rest of the groundbreaking information that would rattle that household forever.

"Firstly, once Popov's daughter was born (Fabiana, in case this information is too much to contain), he started craving something younger. Once she was twelve years old, Popov, with the permission of Carol Farrow, began to rape Fabiana. There was nothing she could do, as it was for the good of the family and it needed to be this way for future success. She was too young to understand how wrong and disgusting that is. She was never allowed to touch me because she always had someone else touching her, and by the grace and kindness of Carol Farrow's heart, she allowed her a break. However, if I could choose any of them to beat me, it would be Fabiana. She has endured far more than the rest of the family combined. In fact, this propaganda that Carol would indoctrinate in her children allowed them to believe there was nothing superior to their household. It was only the Farrows that could withstand any misfortune, whether that be the mysterious and elusive disappearance of their father or the permissible destruction of their dearest Fabiana by the Russian. I mean, gentlemen and women of Quintbridge, Carol Farrow allowed for the rape of her own daughter with her father just because she was so drunken with love and obsession.

"This brainwashing of the children allowed Carol Farrow to complete anything she pleased with almost no consequence. I will only touch on this briefly because I do not want to bring up anything dark in the past. It was by the fault of her children, specifically the complex and dismal character of Jacques and the reluctance of Blanche, that Ms. Kabila died. She died by murder. All Carol Farrow's doing.

"However, if there is anyone eviler by the influence of her mother, it is Fabiana. I don't mean to digress so bluntly in this letter that, if you have read this far, which I am sure most of you have, this girl has done much worse than the murder of Ms. Kabila by some almost adult teenagers like Blanche and Jacques. Although she has never beaten me or psychologically tortured me like Lady Farrow, Fabiana decides to do even worse. She knows things that the rest of us do not. She is highly intelligent. Nobody sees her in the neighborhood because she hides in corners and keeps quiet, but secretly, she observes for weaknesses, whether that process is subconscious or conscious. Carol Farrow always made her sit and watch, forcing her to never interact, giving her the punishment of a night with the Russian if she ever did, and now she has turned into the monster that she is. She has found my weakness and uses it against me to get whatever she wants, whether that be peace and quiet or mindless chores, retaliating at my mother, brother, or sister or perhaps attempting to beat them myself. She knows that I care about her well-being, unlike the rest of her family. She knows I always want to consolidate her when she goes through some painful event like a night with the Russian.

"What she specifically does is this. If she wants something from me, she threatens death. She threatens suicide. She will stare at me directly in the eyes, unflinching and unmoving, and slice the skin on her arms with a blade. She will make sure I will do whatever it is because if not, her death will get pinpointed on me. I would face more abuse and more beatdowns, would be restricted by more rules, and be forced to stay jolly about it to the rest of the community. Finally, she knows I will be traumatized for life. Fabiana, if you happen to be reading this, I hope your corners burn. I hope you burn with them. You stand there, amused, while I get destroyed by my family. This is a choice I never asked for, and yet, you make it more hellish. Everywhere you go, I wish to only be a spotlight on you, allowing everybody in your presence to know you are there. You hurt me more than anyone else could, Fabiana, and that is because you use your extreme and melancholy circumstances to compress me into doing whatever you may find pleasing.

"This letter is already too long for the rest of the neighborhood to read, but I feel as if I must say one last thing before I end it. If there is anyone kind enough to help me and support my decision to leave this family, please reach out. I refuse to go back to that wretched household. Every tulip on that driveway will eventually rot after this family gets sent to prison, and I must avoid the position of watching the rot as best as I could. Help me, dearest neighbors. Please help me. Kindest regards, Cassandra."

CHAPTER XXIV

The children did not speak a word for some time, and Delilah began to cry.

"We had no idea that your family had gone through all of that," said the eldest Ledger.

"Yes, I know. It is quite shocking, but I still need your help. Ledgers, I need you to print it all for me. Sixty copies. With those, I will have the Lillis twins spreading them around. Gabriel and Delilah, do you think it is good how it is?" asked Cassandra

"Yes, we do, but we have a few suggestions. I do think that you should keep some parts of the letter out for the safety of—"

"Let me stop you there, Gabriel. I am not going to change anything. I wanted a simple 'Yes' or 'No' answer from you, and you have given me that. Thank you. Ledgers, when can I get the copies from you?"

"We can get them by the next weekend if that is okay. Our father is busy with one of his jobs at the current moment and will not be free until a week from now."

"That works well with me. I hope everyone is now well-informed because you all can go home now. Thank you for attending."

She watched as everybody got up and left the area. Andra and Jason did not say a word to her as they left. Gabriel and Delilah took turns hugging the girl, and Delilah cried relatively loudly. They too drifted back into the woods toward their homes, as did the Ledger boys. All that remained was Cassandra. She held the letter in her hands, and her straight face looked onward. The pond sat in front of her, still and quiet as the light breeze brushed over the world. She turned to the Lillis twins who still lingered next to her, playing with twigs and stones. They jumped up on the logs, scratching the bark that had stayed put for as long as it had, and tried moving the triangle shape around so that it was a pyramid. She asked them kindly to leave and give her some space for the night.

Their random spurts of laughter coasted through the trees and eventually died down. Cassandra sat down on some of the slimy rocks next to the lake. One had a backrest, and she leaned on it gracefully, putting all her exhaustion onto the rock and absorbing the energy of nature. She looked over to the pond, and back at her paper. She shivered with the cool breeze and chirps in the canopies above her. Her eyes seemed to blur, and her throat swelled. Her straight face turned to a frown, and it seemed as if she could no longer control herself. Streams of tears painted her face, and she only started into the distance, sniffling and crying. She was so utterly sad at her circumstance and felt as if there was truly nothing she could do to fix it. She was aware of the cruelty that came with the letter, but that cruelty was the only answer she had ever known.

She was ready to spread all of this information and get justice for what she endured over these past years. However, as each tear fell down her face, she felt like she was distancing from her original plan. She could only be sad about two things: ruining her reputation and ruining Fabiana's reputation. Her love for her sister made her extremely sad, and she could foresee what was to happen to her if the letter did not work the way she intended. She only lay in sorrowful fright for a few moments, and once the moon was visible and perched above the trees to illuminate the water, Cassandra stood up and went back home.

✳   ✳   ✳

The final slivers of the sun washed the sky a deep pink, and Cassandra admired it before she continued walking toward the Farrow household with Gabriel and Delilah. Only a few hours ago, Cassandra was running between houses, dispensing each of the letters that the Ledger boys had provided her with a day prior. She had darted to each house in each direction from the Farrow household, hoping to elicit the grandest reaction she could so she could receive help. As she elegantly walked down the winding roads of Quintbridge, she saw her old household had a commotion surrounding it. There were crowds of people shouting from all directions, though not a soul stood on the property, and on the steps of her house, Carol Farrow stood screaming.

She yelled at each person who screamed at her, attempting to defend herself from the claims that her actions of abuse, neglect and direct harm were legitimate. Men dressed in uniform, who were the same officers in the case of Ms. Kabila's death, had shown up. They maneuvered through the crowd of people standing and attempted to speak to Carol. Cassandra, Gabriel, and Delilah stood near the crowd, and it only took mere minutes for Carol to spot them.

"Cassandra! Get over here now!" she wailed, almost as if she were a banshee.

"That will not be necessary, Carol," replied the police. She was standing stiffly, her thick legs seeming to be as hard as stone, and she looked at the police with disorientation and bewilderment. She could not believe that she was being restrained from seeing her legal daughter.

Once Lady Farrow screamed for Cassandra to go back to the house, the children inside came bursting out. Jacques and Blanche immediately found Cassandra in the crowd and proclaimed that they will beat her for her crimes against the family. They threatened her with a variety of actions, stating that this treasonous letter she had written will demolish the structure they created. A bowl of celery soup had flown in the air and drowsed Carol Farrow in its green clumps and liquids. It was from an elderly woman, who stated that the Farrow household was a replica of the Devil and the demons.

"You will turn just like Ms. Kabila for that, old hag!" stammered Carol. She slammed her mouth shut with her palm after saying that, fearing that her words could have incriminated her for good. The policemen only stood in shame, unknowing what to do with the situation, and began to usher some of the crowd out of the way and back home.

However, it was Fabiana whom the crowd was forced to stay. She managed to move in front of the policemen and stand there with a knife. She worriedly stared off into the distance, looking for Cassandra.

"Cassandra! Where are you? Come here, please!" she said with her raised voice. Her hand trembled with the knife, and she began hyperventilating. Her eyes quivered back and forth as she waited for the girl to appear. Cassandra, although being protected from the crowd by Gabriel and Delilah, as well as the Candella family, pushed through the crowd and stood a safe distance from the girl. She was nervous for the girl, but everybody urged Cassandra to move back in case the devilish girl was to stab her out of the hatred in her heart that originated from the family. Everybody quietened down to hear what the girl was to say.

"How could you do this to your own sister, Cassandra? How? I have shown nothing but love to you, always! I never kicked you, beat you, or did anything! Why would you do this to me?" cried Fabiana. She frowned and her facial muscles contracted to look like she was in intense pain—but it was only the result of her crying. Her eyes poured tears. People wanted to consolidate her, but the weapon was too much of a risk to get involved with.

"Fabiana, I had to. It was for my own safety. Truth hurts, but it had to be told," replied Cassandra.

"Not in front of the entire neighborhood! You told everybody my secrets, you evil girl!" she replied. She raised her arm with the knife and walked forward, sniffling at every step.

"Fabiana, stop! Don't get any closer!" said Cassandra fearfully. She was truly terrified that Fabiana was going to kill her in front of everybody! She took some steps backward, but Fabiana had stopped moving, just as she had asked. There was no longer the sound of her sniffling; all that stood was Fabiana staring at Cassandra, her hand still raised, and her face blanked with expression. Her cheeks, the same as her mother's, were shining with wet streams of tears. She put the knife to her throat and began to slice it slowly, shaking as blood poured from her neck.

"No! Fabiana, no! Stop! Stop!" exclaimed Cassandra, now rushing to the girl. The crowd shrieked in horror as the young girl began shredding the skin on her neck. Carol Farrow screamed loudly, and fell to her knees, hoping her daughter had not ended her life completely. Half the policemen rushed to the girl as well and quickly ripped some clothes off to stop her bleeding. They took the knife away from the girl and tried to make sure she was still alive. Only a small section of her neck had been cut open, but the blood was showering out of her as if it could not wait to separate from her body entirely. She looked lifeless but returned her eyes to the police officer. The noise of crying and screaming faded in her ears, and she only muttered some quiet sentences. "Everything in the letter is t-t-true."

"Carol Farrow, you are under arrest. Do not speak a word," said the policeman as he made his way toward the woman. She did not speak, only cried, and did not open her eyes. The policemen quickly rushed Fabiana to a doctor, hoping that she lives from the deadly cut.

"Come with me, kind girl. You may live with us temporarily before we can officially send you to an orphanage to be re-adopted by us again. We are so sorry, Cassandra… sweet, sweet girl. We are so sorry," said Lady Candella. She hugged the girl tightly, avoiding touching her wide eyes that only focused on her sister who lay covered in blood.

They carried Cassandra away toward their home. In a few hours, the policemen knocked on the Candella household and asked if they

148

could protect and keep Cassandra there for the while. They prepared a meal for the girl that night—potatoes and cabbages, as well as a perfectly cooked hunk of beef, seasoned with oranges, salt, and butter— but Cassandra did not take a single bite. The dining room was quiet, where only the clinks of forks and fine china dinnerware sliced through the air.

"Cassandra, sweety, you must eat something," said the Candella woman. She looked at her husband, concerned. Cassandra did not reply to them, only staring at the ground somewhere. The Candella woman turned to Delilah, who also sat at the dining table, filling her face with the dinner. "Delilah, stop eating so much. It is beyond rude considering that the girl across from you has a sister who could be dead. You mustn't be presented as a fool when you are not. Now, say some words to the girl and make sure she eats something," whispered the woman to her daughter.

Delilah felt uncomfortable at the request for her to stop eating, however, she did as her mother asked. She subtly cleared her throat and wiped the corners of her mouth before she nervously spoke to the girl.

"Cassandra? Cassandra? Are you listening?" asked Delilah. Cassandra's eyes darted toward the girl, not moving her head but only focusing her intense stare on the girl.

"I think you should eat something. I know your family is in a troubling situation right now, but I don't believe starving yourself will make you feel better. Please eat something." Delilah turned to her parents in proud delight, thinking she had magically solved the issue of Cassandra not eating anything. Nobody moved or made noise, except for the stretch of Delilah's clothes while she turned to her parents and the exhale of her father.

"For such a smart girl, you are so ignorant," Cassandra muttered. Delilah seemed stunned at the comment, and her parents were shocked at the sudden insult of the girl. The Candella parents believed that there was a deep friendship between them, but this comment made them reevaluate what they thought.

Delilah stood up from her seat and stared angrily at Cassandra. "Sit down!" whispered the mother, grabbing her daughter's arm. Delilah shook it off. Cassandra sat straight up before turning to face Cassandra where they interlocked eye contact for a few moments.

"All I have ever been to you is nice and kind, Cassandra. We were friends before I started hanging out with the Shabah boy across the neighborhood, and suddenly, you have ostracized me from everything we have ever had. You no longer talk to me, and I am sick of it! Now, by my request, we have invited you to our home before you are sent to another orphanage to be readopted by someone. That 'someone' is probably going to be us again, considering we are the only family who not only can support another child adequately but also cares about you. Stop being the spoiled Farrow daughter you were raised to be and start being grateful for the people that care about you... me. Start being grateful for me!"

"Do you really think I am not grateful for your family? I am endlessly grateful. There is no other place I would rather be. However, you have made it impossible for gratefulness. I would rather be anywhere but with a prostitute like you who cannot help but undermine her own intelligence with her impulsive and stupid actions! Sorry that I have come to seek and communicate the truth, and I am sorry if I offend you—but right now, in this very moment, I cannot stand you! My sister is possibly dead, and you are screaming at me! Shut it, Delilah... legs, and mouth!"

Delilah gasped at this comment and picked up a fistful of hot beef to through at the girl. Her clothes were stained in animal oils and reeked of orangey meats.

"Not in my house! Delilah, get out! Go out the door and sit outside for an hour!" demanded the mother, furious at the childish action of her daughter.

"But mother, it's cold! Why are you yelling at me when Cassandra caused all of this?"

"I will address my daughter first. Blood always comes first. Now go!" she replied. Cassandra looked down when she heard the comment and swallowed, feeling as if the anxiety of the situation had finally axed her apart.

"Cassandra, how gross you are! Change your clothes immediately. Also, if you ever speak about my child or this family in any sort of negative manner again, I will have your tongue and this hospitality will discontinue. Go wash up."

Unbeknownst to Cassandra, this family was better than anything she had ever experienced. The only reason she acted the way she did was that that was the only way she knew how to interact with the family. The Candella household was bound to fortify her soul and her personality with grace, kindness, and sternness. She felt equally excited and nervous about what the next few months would look like before she entered an orphanage again, but she would never discern these feelings because of her blinding hatred for Delilah. She was plagued by the one thing she wished to have more than ever: a boy. She felt as if she would perhaps hate Delilah forever for stealing the one thing she wanted more than anything else.

CHAPTER XXV

On the mystical night of an early November date, Gabriel had personally requested to go by horseback to the center of town with Delilah, where Penelope's Cafe was.

It was an exotic scene, filled with neutral tones and oranges, and sprinkled with hints and lines of green, as well as dusted with pots of large elephant's ear plants. It had wooden seats that surrounded cute round tables, and small mats covered the floors with vibrant colors. The workers were instructed to walk around the cafe, dressed in professional suits and accepting requests for water or coffee refills. It smelled of deep pumpkin and cinnamon. Penelope was working there too, casually walking to different groups of people who were eating or drinking and asking them if they are enjoying their time. She was a petite old lady, always holding her hands behind her back and keeping a full head of hair. Her rocky voice, subsisting of wrinkles, age, and wisdom, made people cheerful and welcomed any stranger. Penelope decided to take on the calming job of restaurant owner after years of working for an oil tycoon—whom she nicknamed kitty—and successfully keeping a stable income that could last her centuries. She appreciated her cafe more than people imagined, and she was aware of the reputation it had created around town.

In the corner of every wall, there were romantic lanterns flying and hovering about, as well as another unlit lantern and some paints on each table-for-two for couples to send their best wishes to Penelope's ceiling. Penelope personalized each of the paintings in the cafe too, ranging from remakes of classic paintings and some abstract ones. Jazz music always played on a stage in the background where a band was performing. Gabriel knew this place was going to be the place where Delilah and he were to kiss for the first time. They had officially been dating for quite some time, and now was the time more than ever.

In the mirage of the lanterns and plants, Gabriel and Delilah sat at a table for two. While Delilah used the reds and the blues to configure some small artistic paintings of themselves, Gabriel was planning the best way to lean in and make the move. He ordered an assortment of fruits and a cake, and Delilah ordered some juice as well as some bread and butter. Her delicate nature charmed Gabriel even more, and after the many months of hurt and torture that they had endured, he could no longer help but make sure that their relationship was solidified.

Their dinner ended quite quickly, and just as they lit the lantern, Gabriel leaned in and planted a kiss on her lips. It was as if a nuclear surge of energy was going to burst out of their chests, considering their situation. They knew it would be love.

In the window, three young girls frolicked in the center of town. A girl peered in the window intensely, thinking that she could recognize someone in there. The friends of the girl also stopped before turning to the girl and asking: "Is that Gabriel and Delilah? Are they kissing?" Cassandra could only respond with watery eyes and a soft agreement before they quickly skipped away, pretending as if the reality they saw was not, in fact, reality.

The girls settled by the side of a fountain, watching the water ripple its minuscule waves against the stone. A magnificent statue stood in the center of the spout, and one girl found it particularly interesting.

"Would it be a bad idea if I jumped inside the water?" asked Gisella, one of the girls.

"Yes, it would. Please do not do that, Gisella," responded Cassandra. "Do you know what is exceptionally frustrating? Gabriel and I met first, and I really thought we would end up together. I even created a scrapbook page for him before he caught me in the window. I just feel as if we are meant for each other. Then I introduced him to my pretty, amazing, smart friend Delilah, thinking he would be impressed that I could be friends with someone as fantastic as her, but he was only impressed with her the entire time. I am just so frustrated at how stupid I was! Did I really think that he would like me more if I showed him someone better? Am I that delirious? What do you girls think?"

"Honestly," began Shytone, the other girl, "I think that you should not worry about him any longer. He clearly does not want you, and you are gorgeous. You must look for another boy. The only hope you have is another boy because you have been officially adopted by the Candella family and you are going to be reminded that they are together constantly."

"Well, what if I try and do revenge? What if I sabotage them?" asked Cassandra.

"If I am going to tell you the truth, that would only remind me of your mother—old mother, I mean." Cassandra did not respond to that, but only exhaled before standing on her legs quickly.

"We should all swim in the fountain. We only live once, so why not?" she said with a bright smile. All the girls laughed and dove into the water, not caring about how disgusting it could possibly be but only wanting to have some impulsive fun.

After an hour, Gabriel opened the door for Delilah to leave the cafe. They did not get to speak to Penelope this time, but they were sure that they would come back and see her. It would be a historic day for the couple, and as they made their way toward Quintbridge, they hoped that they wouldn't have to leave. They hoped that there would be some extraneous event that leads to them staying together that night. Delilah did have a Spanish event tomorrow morning, however, and she knew she could not stay any minute longer.

Gabriel dropped her off at her home before walking back to his house, where he heard faint screams. Nervous that something detrimental could have happened to his mother, he quickly ran inside, concerned and yelling. His mother ran towards him smiling and jumping, embracing him in her arms.

"Gabriel you would not believe this! I just got the news that the Victoriana couple had gambled all their money and won back everything they had lost! They might even buy the house back from the girls that live in it now. How very exciting!" she screamed

They were all ecstatic to hear such good news, considering how much loss the Victoriana couple had endured. They knew that the Victoriana couple deserved to be in this neighborhood more than anyone else could ever, and now that they finally have enough money to come back, they will. It was only a matter of deciding which house they were to buy: their original house or the Farrow house. They thought about taking revenge in that aspect but were unsure.

CHAPTER XXVI

A court case had arisen in Quintbridge.

After the banishment of Lady Farrow, and after all the children were put under the care of a governmental supervisor until a decision could be reached, the Victoriana couple had reaffirmed their position as leaders of the neighborhood. They reclaimed their household from the women, who were, in exchange, promised the Farrow household once the children are allowed to leave. Nobody minded the women, who were completely absorbed in their own business and could not care to interfere with the affairs of their neighbors. It would be quite refreshing for the residents to have a new face in that house after so many years of Farrow's residing.

The Victoriana couple sued Lady Farrow for defamation, and the perfect evidence was present through the letters they had kept. All that would need to happen in the trial is for Lady Farrow to be asked to write in her handwriting, and the letters would match.

After a short period of time, when the crescent of Christmas was upon the country, the Victorianas became successful in their trial. They hoped to receive a large sum of money from the woman, but they were not gifted with such and were only awarded ten thousand dollars. They were still content with the fact that the law agreed with their perspective of the issue regardless of their intended financial gain. Lady Farrow had now been despised by the entire neighborhood that it would be impossible for her to rebound if she was ever to come back from jail.

The Victoriana couple had made strides unlike anyone else in the neighborhood. There was a certain drive they had to achieve everything they possibly could, and although they were raised in an atmosphere of old money, they realized how to attain the same wealth. Their abundance of luck was ultimately the deciding factor. However, with this deciding factor for success came the realization of the deciding factor of failure. Communication with members of the neighborhood is what damaged them so badly, considering that there is no possible way to navigate where someone's intentions lie.

A formal vow of silence was received by all members of the neighborhood, save the Candella family and the Shabah family. There was absolutely no return from this, and they considered their vow to be the next pure step toward success as residents. The only thing the Victoriana couple was excited about was starting over as the opposite of what they were before. Nobody knew what they wanted, but it is quite simple. The Victorianas wanted to spend the rest of their time in their own space and world, where no dramatic slanders existed. They would always be quiet and humble in this world, and that was the only true way happiness could be derived for them.

On Christmas eve, Andra asked for only one gift which was absurdly strange for her. Usually, the girl would force her way into upwards of thirty gifts for Christmas, feeling as if she never had enough. She cared more about the number of gifts than the actual gifts in themselves.

"Mother, I request only a single thing. I have wanted this ever since I was a child, but I have never formally asked for it before. I wish to go to school. I no longer appreciate the private tutors of languages and algebra, as well as science, history, and poetry. I want to experience what a real school is like, considering that there is not much else for me to do here. Gabriel is going to finish schooling entirely soon, and I feel that I will get lonely if I am not allowed to go. Also, I have no other friends here. My only friend with that I have established a pure friendship was Jason, but of course, I cannot speak to him again. That is the only thing I ask of you, dear mother."

Ms. Shabah felt confused about this proposal but thought it was quite easy to do. It was much easier than pleasing Andra with a bounty of complicated gifts that she won't care about for longer than two days. She had enrolled her in the school closest by, which was the Quintbridge School for Boys and Girls. It was well-respected, and it allowed a majority of students to succeed. The gold rusher built this school, and it laid the foundation for other successful pioneers in the Quintbridge realm, so she felt it necessary to allow her.

On Christmas day, Gabriel received a small batch of seven gifts—five of which were for his Delilah. The others consisted of a new toothbrush and a cup of mint to make sure his breath was clean and healthy, as well as a new diary since he had stopped journaling earlier in the year. His immediate stop was because of the distracting nature of the neighborhood—constantly keeping his thoughts busy. Delilah was also an easy outlet to express everything he thought honestly and without shame. After months of spending time with her and her family, he had become accustomed to confidently using the Spanish language as he had acquired most of it from listening to conversations and having Delilah translate them for him afterward. "Dios mío, estoy cansado de estar aguantando esta mujer," he would say each time his mother spoke about his future with Delilah. He liked when she laughed at his remarks, and often at dinner, he would say, "esta cena me da asci, como me gustaría comer pastel por el estanque." It was as if he was speaking a secret language that only he and Delilah could understand since his mother was clueless.

Andra did not receive anything save the exciting news of her enrollment in the nearby school. She was ecstatic and immediately began making plans for what she should wear and do at school, as well as who she wants to meet when she gets there.

✻   ✻   ✻

Andra was placed in advanced courses in philosophy, English language, and calculus, at the request of her mother. She had made sure that Andra was receiving the best formal education she could muster, considering she was no longer being taught by the maidens and tutors that Ms. Shabah would hire.

As if it were instant, Andra came to realize that Delilah was exceedingly smarter than everyone else. She always thought her snobbish attitude and creepy love for her brother would blemish her intelligence, but she was quite mistaken. Delilah knew absolutely every answer to every question that could possibly be asked. When the teacher did not have any volunteers for an answer, or if none of the students could give the correct response, he relied on her. She eloquently spoke in front of her peers, impressing both the teacher and the other students. Her reputation of being the smartest girl alive had become fluid throughout the entire school, and she was sought for answers to a variety of tests, homework, and assignments. It was not until Andra came to realize that there was a reluctance that Delilah had—resulting from a deep fear of getting her wrist whacked by the ruler—to share answers, so nobody could truly get them out of her.

When it was time for the first partner project, all the students flew to Delilah, hoping that she could partner with them. Once she chose her pick—Shytone, a friend of Cassandra's—she settled in her seat and demanded everybody leave her alone. The reason she chose Shytone is because of the girl's unfortunate condition of stupidity, where she simply cannot and will not understand any sort of academic material. Cassandra was there too, partnered with Gisella.

Andra was lost on who to pick for her partner. Each person scurried around her, and she felt as if she would be on the brink of trample, but she caught a familiar face in the distance sitting alone and staring at her. Jason's eyes twinkled in the reflection of the window, entrapping the easily manipulative Andra. She found her way walking toward him—the banished boy whom she could never speak to again—so that she could ask him to be her partner.

"Well, hello stranger. I have not seen you in a while—thought you could have died," said Jason in his humorous, sly tone.

"Well, of course not. And you should not joke about the death—not while Cassandra is still here. Yes, she is a maniac, but I would still appreciate people giving her respect during what she has gone through. I'm pretty sure she is either in the orphanage now or staying with the Candella family. Anyways, that is beside the point. Would you, Jason Grealm, please be my partner? I have no one else left."

"Of course, dear. There is no one else I would rather work with. Why have I not seen you in a while?"

"My mother has banished me from seeing you ever again, as you may know. If you did not know, now you know. It is also difficult to meet you when there aren't any events anymore. The bonfire was the last time I saw you. Now, that won't be the last. I go to *school* now, and we have plenty of time to be with each other when we want."

Jason creased his mouth with a smile, unable to move his fixed eyes from the girl. While they chatted about the partner project, Jason only thought about how there is going to be more of a relationship now that Andra is allowed to leave her home. There was a peculiar sense that everything was going to work out inside of him—a hope that he could not discern the meaning and origin.

For weeks, Cassandra woke up an extra fifteen minutes to get ready for her school day and arrive there earlier than expected. She also stayed an extra fifteen minutes. It puzzled her mother, Ms. Shabah, who wondered what the girl was going so early for and why she had to stay later than expected.

Andra told her mother that there is a secret chemistry club for women, and she decided to join since she has taken a huge liking to chemistry. She blamed her infatuation with the subject on Delilah, who, by her genius intellect, has planted a seed of passion inside her brain. It was quite exciting for Ms. Shabah to hear that the school has turned her into a zealous learner.

She has also told her mother that she has now regained her friendship with Cassandra and a few of her friends: Gisella, a loud girl who always wore iridescent clothes, Kelleen, a very quiet girl who only spoke with Cassandra, and another quiet girl named Shytone. She and Shytone would make their way towards chemistry club rendezvous before and after school each day, and when they were there, the president of the club—another girl named Sophia—would scold them for being late. She mentioned this to her mother in order to extend the time she could have to go to school. In reality, the chemistry club did not exist, and neither did Sophia, the scolding president. She never spoke with Shytone, Kelleen, or Gisella, and in fact, only spoke with Jason. Occasionally, Delilah and she exchanged some words about how the school is, how smart Delilah is, or how Andra is not doing anything with Jason. That was a trick she liked to employ to gaslight Delilah—it was not working—about their relationship.

Ms. Shabah was hesitant on allowing her to have an extension and decided to consider asking Delilah that evening for her input. "Andra, sweet child, I think I will talk about the extension tonight at dinner. Gabriel and Delilah are coming to join us, and I think I should ask their opinion of the club to see if they like the idea."

Andra panicked at the thought of Delilah exposing her lies to Ms. Shabah, and quickly came up with something to tell to keep anything from being ruined. "Oh, mother, that won't be necessary. It is not that urgent to extend my time at all. We don't have to get anyone else involved," she said quickly and nervously.

"Nonsense, my sweet! I don't want you to continue getting scolded by this rude and obnoxious Sophia girl. We will sort it out tonight," responded Ms. Shabah.

Andra smiled at her mother joyfully, before going back upstairs to her room and pacing back and forth. She was frightened of what was to happen but decided to calm down. She thought of one tactic that would actually work: distracting everybody as soon as the chemistry club was mentioned. She was sure that this would work and that there would be no further discussion about this. Now that she was finally happy with her life and she had Jason again, she refused to let her wicked lies destroy everything she had created.

Within an hour, Delilah arrived at the front door of the Shabah household. Gabriel let her inside and noticed it was snowing outside.

The small flakes dotted the grass in small patches of white, generating a merry mood that would foreshadow the dinner.

"Welcome, Delilah! We are so thrilled to have you for tonight," said Ms. Shabah, giving her a warm hug. There was a sense of security entangled in the woman that allowed all her guests to feel as if they entered their own homes.

"Thank you, Ms. Shabah. I appreciate your kindness, and I cannot wait for this delicious dinner," she said with a curtsey. Ms. Shabah led her into the dining room, where a candlelit roast was playing out on the table. Ms. Shabah sat at one side of the head of the table with Gabriel across her, and Delilah and Andra sat across each other.

"So, Delilah, how is school going for you?" asked Ms. Shabah.

"It's quite good. I am still getting stellar grades, and everything seems to be going smoothly. Andra is in my class too, which is nice. It is always good to see some familiar company there. She is also picking up all the subjects quite well," said Delilah.

"Well, that is good to hear. I always knew my daughter was smart."

"Yes, indeed, Cassandra is very intelligent. Far more intelligent than most other people in there," said Delilah as she smiled at Andra. She smiled back, hoping that nothing else gets brought up.

"I heard she is taking a liking to chemistry—of all subjects! She also joined a secret women's club for chemistry. Are you in it, dear?" asked Ms. Shabah.

"Oh, mother, look! The tree outside looks as if it is about to fall!" yelled Andra, hoping to distract them from speaking any further. Everyone got up and looked outside to see the tree.

"Which tree are you talking about? They all look quite sturdy to me, Andra," said Gabriel.

"Oh, it must have been a hallucination. I think I have a headache, mother. A very painful one," said Andra in a distressed tone of voice. She tried acting as best she could to distract them.

"Go drink some water, Andra. It is probably dehydration, which could be deadly. Quickly, go! We will resume our conversation while you are gone," said Ms. Shabah.

"No, don't. I think the thought of school makes my head hurt," she said. The group laughed, thinking Andra was making jokes. She seemed extremely concerned about what would happen.

"Go drink, Cassandra Shabah. Now!" demanded her mother.

"Okay, mother, I will. Relax," said Andra. She rushed to go get water, took only one sip, and ran back. After all, she was not telling the truth about her extreme headache.

"So, back to what we were talking about. Have you joined the secret women's club for chemistry, Delilah?" asked Ms. Shabah. Once she finished her sentence, Andra ran back to sit down, insisting on how much better she felt from the few sips of water.

"I'm glad to hear you are feeling better, Andra, but no, Ms. Shabah, I have not heard of such a club," responded Delilah.

"Well, of course, you cannot know of it. It is a *secret* club," remarked Andra.

"Yes, that is true, Andra. It is led by that Sophia girl, whom Andra says is quite rude and snaps at her when she is late to the meetings in the morning and after school. Do you know of her behavior?" asked Ms. Shabah. Andra muttered a terrified "No" under her breath when she heard the name Sophia be brought up.

"Interesting. We do not have a Sophia at the school," said Delilah. The room grew silent, and Ms. Shabah stared disappointingly at her daughter. Delilah spoke again to try and rid the silence. "Oh wait, I think there is a Sophia. I had no idea that she was passionate about Chemistry, though. She told me she is more of a philosophy girl and is engaging in debates with her family at dinner."

"Yes, she is quite a peculiar girl," asserted Andra quietly. They did not speak for a few minutes while they gnawed on some potatoes and enjoyed their sliced pork. Delilah proclaimed this is one of the best meals she has had since being with Gabriel, which caused Ms. Shabah to blush at her compliment.

"Also, I just thought I should mention, I am really delighted by this change in mood within the neighborhood. A few weeks ago, the atmosphere was so dismal, and now I can't help but feel as if all problems have just dissipated into thin air like they never existed. I mean, Andra and Jason are close again at school, which I never expected to happen! I'm glad we are all changing for the better—less drama and more of a positivist attitude to things," said Delilah, smiling at everyone at the table. When her eyes met Andra, she saw how petrified she looked, as if there was a knife to her throat, she confusedly furrowed her eyebrows.

"Excuse me, what?" asked Ms. Shabah, dropping her fork and knife and turning to look at her daughter. Andra avoided all sense of eye contact with the woman and faced the ground. Her eyes began tearing up, and she felt as if there was something terrible about to happen.

"Yes, Jason and Andra are friends again. They talk every day, and if I am not mistaken, I believe they could be dating. How cute they are!" said Delilah, unsure of what all the fuss was about.

"Delilah, dear, thank you for telling me this," began Ms. Shabah. "I obviously had no idea about any of this information whatsoever. Cassandra Shabah, look at me now." Andra turned to face the woman, horrified at what she is going to do. "I am going to say this calmly and quietly so that my anger is not expressed in front of our guest, Delilah. There will be absolutely no negotiations because this is as solid as it will get. There is no watering down this statement. You are to be pulled out of school tomorrow, you will never speak to Jason Grealm ever again, and you will be receiving your education. I want you to honestly tell me something, and if you lie, I will send you back to an orphanage just like the poor girl who lived across the street. Is this chemistry club real? Is Sophia real? Are you friends with Kelleen, Gisella, and Shytone? Answer those questions for me."

"No, mother, none of those things I said were true. I lied to you about them all. I am so sorry, but—"

"No 'buts,' Cassandra. Thank you for being honest. You will never speak to any of those people, anyways, since your last day at school is today. Jason Grealm will not exist in your mind or any other Shabah mind again. Once you turn twenty years of age, you can make your own decisions about what to do with your life. Lucky for me, Jason will not be interested in you by that age. You are also forbidden to tell this boy what has happened to you. I cannot believe you would lie to my face, break the loyalty and trust we created over never talking to the Grealm family again, and then hide the truth from me. I am beyond disappointed in you, Andra. Beyond."

Andra did not say anything in return. She ate nothing else on her plate, letting the meat and potatoes go cold. Ms. Shabah continued the conversation with Delilah and Gabriel as if that discussion was minor and nothing but a rule that had to be reinstated. Cassandra Shabah cried tears of silver, washing her face from the sin she had done with the salty drops of her eyes. She had never experienced such dread in her life. Her lips pattered as if she were about to mumble something quietly.

"You are the worst mother I have ever known."

CHAPTER XXVII

"JULY 31, 1902. I have decided to begin dating my journal entries now. I feel as if this might be the best one yet. I cannot wait to break the news to mother, since I know this is all she would want. Cassandra is still not perfectly good. She has refused to feel better about her circumstances since the conversation at dinner about the Grealm family. Why does it even matter to her anymore? She could do so much better than that pathetic low life with a prostitute mother. I'm so happy with my Delilah. I think we might get married. Quintbridge was truly a blessing in disguise. I am beyond surprised at how my life has turned out since the two years of living here. I cannot wait for my next chapter in life, whatever goodness that may be. If I am to give one piece of advice to my older self—if future Gabriel is ever reading this, it is to stay faithful. The good will always transcend the evil. I promise you that, future Gabriel."

Gabriel put the ink away inside his desk along with his diary that he had gotten for Christmas two years ago. He was excited to visit the market with his mother, sister, and his dearest Delilah. He rushed to the carriage they had prepared and greeted his family. They rode by Delilah's house, where she stood waving. She wore a pleasant blue dress, covered with a floral pattern. She looked pulchritudinous; more elegant than any other woman he had ever seen. He dazzled her.

She sat next to him in the carriage, excited to visit the market and see some of the exotic new fruits and vegetables they were selling there. Andra was still sulking, wishing she was not present, and Ms. Shabah was extremely happy for the young couple.

When they arrived at the market, it seemed like all of Quintbridge was there. The place was bustling with people, and the sellers enthusiastically exchanged their goods for money. Women were walking out with handfuls of goods that they had purchased, men were drinking and smoking nearby, and everybody seemed cheerful. The carriage stopped and each of them walked out, soaking in the atmosphere of the people around them.

"It surely is a pleasant sight!" exclaimed Delilah.

"Yes, it is," said Gabriel in agreement.

They walked through the markets until they reached a large table of tomatoes and carrots. Ms. Shabah wanted to buy at least a few pounds worth of these vegetables for the stew she was planning for the night and asked for Delilah to help with picking them. She also sent Gabriel and Cassandra to find any sort of lamb for the stew so that they could incorporate some fulfilling nutrients along with the stew.

"Ms. Shabah, Gabriel, and I have been meaning to tell you something important," said Delilah as she picked through the vegetables.

"What is it, darling?"

"Well, there is no ease into this, so I must say it how it is. I am pregnant!" she said. Ms. Shabah was utterly shocked at the news that she had dropped her vegetables while she hugged Delilah and rejoiced. The woman managing the stand with the vegetables clapped after eavesdropping on the news.

"How exciting! I have always hoped Gabriel and you would have a child together! I also do hope there is a marriage soon, but that is a proposition for Gabriel to make. Oh, goodness, how blessed we are! I am so happy for you, Delilah. We must celebrate soon!"

"Thank you, kind woman. I have always admired your kind words. There is other news, too—" said Delilah before being interrupted by Gabriel and Andra's appearance. "Oh, well you are back! I just told Ms. Shabah about my pregnancy!"

"What? You're pregnant?" asked Andra, holding a hunk of lamb that was sealed in some paper.

"Yes, Andra. We are beyond excited to begin this new chapter in our lives," she responded. "There is other news, too. Gabriel, would you please speak on it?"

"Sure. We decided we are moving to Fiddlefield again. We saw a flyer about a sizeable ranch out there, and it would be nice to move back to my roots. What do you think?"

"Oh, yes, absolutely. That sounds like a splendid idea," said Ms. Shabah in full support.

"Oh, don't be ridiculous!" said Andra in retaliation. "There are far better places to go, and Fiddlefield is one of the worst. I would rather Quintbridge than that place. Don't go there, you two."

"Cassandra, shut your mouth. It is a fantastic idea. Do what you please, my son. I know that you know what is best for you, and I am excited to see you grow and mature as a man," said Ms. Shabah.

Cassandra looked back to the ground, remembering what her mother thinks of her. She was ready to go home and waited for the conversations about the greatness Gabriel and Delilah were to achieve to end.

In an hour, Delilah was dropped off at her home along with Gabriel and Ms. Shabah went back to her house with her daughter. Cassandra put the vegetables away for her mother while she worked on the lamb. They were excited about the feast that night and hoped their preparation was going to reward them with a delicious lamb stew.

"I am so happy for them. She is practically my daughter," muttered Ms. Shabah. Cassandra overheard her mother speaking to herself and she asked her what she was saying, knowing good and well what she was talking about. She wanted her question to come off as if she could not hear the instruction her mother had given and was intrigued to see if her mother would tell her the truth.

"Nothing, Andra. It is not worth speaking with you about, considering your crippling and chronic negative attitude. Remember, the Arabic tutor is coming tomorrow, so prepare yourself for the lessons. No more speaking to me," she said.

"I know what you said, mother. I heard you clearly, and now you are speaking absurdly to me," Andra said in retaliation. "I was not meaning to be negative today, by the way. I was just shocked by what she said, and I don't want Gabriel to leave my side because then I will be sad. That is all."

"I will not have you speak to me this way, Delilah!"

"Delilah?"

"No! I meant Andra—"

"I cannot believe you! I am always brought to disgust and hatred when you speak mother. I do not care if this is inappropriate, because you need to hear it. I am so fed up with everything that has happened, and the fact that you just called me Delilah just contributes to everything I have against you. I am a woman fueled by anger. I will not accept this abuse by you any longer. You have made my malleable personality miserable!" Andra was now crying excessively as if every emotion she could elicit was building up over the last two years and was finally released in a single burst.

Ms. Shabah stared at her for a few moments, before walking one step closer. The air was stale, and it felt as if there was a dark presence about to swallow the girl whole. Her mother grinned at her before softly speaking. "Arabic tomorrow, Cassandra."

She ran to her room, sobbing loudly and without any sort of fear of being found out as a sad girl. She faced the sky with tears streaming down her face. How cruel her mother was to her! She was immensely jealous of her brother, wishing for nothing but a stable life. She yearned to leave for Fiddlefield too but knew she could not until she was older.

"God, if you are listening, please release me from my mother's awful grasp. I am not a Cassandra like the Farrow girl. I am Cassandra Shabah. Please, God, let me live happily, without hatred of my own mother. Please, God, please!"

THE END

Made in the USA
Middletown, DE
01 March 2023

26008183R00102